Tale

A Short Story Collection

By:

B T Litell

Cover art and illustrations by Bobooks via fiverr.com
Edited by Megan Hundley

First Published in 2021

Visit my website at https://btlitellauthor.com for more details about my writing. Also, follow me on social media to stay up to date on my writing progress. I also stream on Twitch at twitch.tv/bran_muffin91 where I showcase my writing, editing, and even play games!

ISBN: 9781686855320
Kindle ASIN: B08RDRJPT4

Write to
B T Litell
PO Box 274
Canal Winchester, OH 43110

Acknowledgments

I would like to personally acknowledge everyone who has helped me out with getting these short stories written, edited, compiled, and published. First and foremost, my wonderful wife, Mariana, has continued to support me through all of our storms and periods of calm. I truly could do none of this without you and every day I am beyond thankful for your presence, support, love, and mirth in my life, even on days when I don't necessarily show it in ways that I should. You are the reason I started writing again and the reason I continue to write.

To my writing mentor, Rachel, I would like to say thank you from the bottom of my heart for all the help, guidance, and advice that you provide for me throughout my writing journey. I doubt that anyone has contributed as much to my writing as you have and I want to just take a moment to thank you for being there to answer all my questions, make me laugh, and provide light through the darkness to guide me to safety.

To my test readers—there are too many to name personally—I cannot do this without the feedback you provide me. You have been helping me grow as a writer with each story I send you. Thank you all so much.

To my editor, Megan, you have shaped many of these stories and I want to say thank you for all the times you continue to let me send you stories despite the many flaws I have in my writing. Sorry for all the em-dashes I have used instead of commas and my other repeated errors that have likely made you want to pull hair out. Thank you so much for showing me my flaws and helping me correct them.

My cover artists, Cherie Fox and Rafaela, I truly cannot say how much I appreciate the talent both of you have and bring to the table. Your artistic dreams and skills are what have brought my stories to life, maybe as much as the words themselves. I love the designs and want to continue using your brilliant gifts for as long as I am writing stories worthy of your art.

And last but not least, to my readers, I really cannot do any of this without you. Thank you so much for your continued support through every step of my writing journey. It means so much that you would pick up my books once, twice, or however many times it happens to be. Thank you all so much!

Fallen Stars

Chapter One

A gentle breeze rushed across the tops of the forest below a dome-topped tower before it lifted into an open window of the tower's observatory. The gust coming through the window danced a moment with the beard of an Elf standing behind his telescope. His gaze broken, distracted by the moving of his beard, the Elf scratched at his hairy chin. His beard was of medium length and a generous mixture of brown, red, and grey. While the Elf tried his best to keep his beard well-maintained there were lots of stray, curly hairs sticking out everywhere. He returned his eyes to the lens cup of the telescope and returned to admiring the sky. Observing. Studying. Pondering.

The brass edges of the eyepiece, which was a gift from the dwarves, stung his face with the coldness. The observatory dome took on a dull sheen, there above the forest. The Elf watched over the treetops as a vast dark blanket over the world was pierced by pinholes of light. Stars. So far away. Yet they brought some amounts of light. *How long had they been there? What worlds lay beyond this one? Are there other worlds farther still?* So man questions the Elf hoped to answer.

Many thought he was mad wanting to find answers to life as they knew it within the sky, yet he persisted. No one from the nearby towns or villages came to visit, to bother him, to disturb his life's work. His was a hermit's life. Even the two nearby villages, called him "the hermit." Some *wanted* company would not be considered bad or a nuisance. He sought answers. Knowledge. Wisdom. What he sought must be among the stars. He had spent years searching for the answers in the world around him, to no avail. This was the only logical choice that remained.

Already he had learned the moon, others called it the night-sun, orbited their own world. It moved through the sky with an unseen grace, its path changed ever so slightly each night with a slight rotation that was slower than the world's own. He had written a book on the subject, but only a handful of others had asked to read it. Then they argued his findings, without any knowledge of the subject, and claimed not to understand what he had meant when he corrected them.

A glint of light flashed in the sky, and the Elf swung the telescope to inspect the sudden change. Many objects, round in shape, and larger than small mountains had appeared out of nowhere. Fire enveloped the objects, which rapidly grew closer.

The heavens were sending something to the world, something with answers and perhaps more questions too. A closer examination showed seven of these objects, each identical in size but not color. One red, one green, one…yellow. *Or is that the fire around it?* the Elf thought. One white, another blue. One was so dark it could only be identified by the fire ringing it. The last was orange, the color of leaves falling from a tree during harvest. *Spectacular.* As the objects came closer, they seemed to grow farther apart, each one leaving the others as rapidly as they approached the ground. The scientist left his telescope briefly to grab a map and a quill. *I will be* damned *if anyone else discovers one of them before I do.*

One of the orbs, the white one, crashed into the distant mountain range, bringing down an entire mountain with it. *The dwarves will surely find that one.* The dwarves lived in the mountains, their faces and hands covered in dirt, or so tales told. He had only seen a Dwarf once when he got the viewing glass for his telescope. *That* Dwarf had not been covered head to toe in dirt.

Another orb crashed far to the north, another to the east beyond the horizon. One flew over the observatory, the fire surrounding it warming the facility as it passed. Then the cold breeze returned. *It has to be close.* The ground shook, and stones from the roof fell around the hermit as he jotted the orb's positions on the map. The flagstone loosened from the ceiling, and many stones around it fell without their support. Hurriedly, the hermit left his observatory just as most of the ceiling collapsed where he had been standing. *My research!* All that time spent observing the sky, gone. *This discovery will surely make up for that.* He ran down the stairs and into the field behind the observatory. He could see the smoldering trail the orb had left as it skidded across the ground.

Chapter Two

As the sun started rising the next morning, the hermit discovered where the object landed. Many others gathered there, as well. In fact, a crowd formed around the crater, gasping and pointing, wildly and loudly, unsure what this object was that just fell from the sky. The object still radiated far too much heat to get closer than a few hundred yards, and a lot of fires had formed along the ground after it crashed. Thankfully, most of the fires had been at least contained. The Elf used a spyglass, one of his more practical inventions, gazing at the object. As he had seen through the telescope, the object, now broken into many scattered pieces, was a large jewel-like orb, very nearly perfect in its roundness. It was blue in color, the outer parts of the blue stone were translucent, and a bright light shone through, almost shining as bright as the sun. Somehow the blue shell dimmed its light enough that bystanders could look at it without having to shield their eyes.

"What is it?" someone asked the hermit from the crowd.

Annoying simpletons. They always want answers to things handed to them instead of finding their own answers. "I'm trying to discern that, but your constant chatter is disturbing my studies," the Elf replied. *Such nuisances.*

While staring at the orb, the Elf noticed a small chunk, slightly bigger than his own fist, that had broken off and landed a couple dozen yards in front of where the crowd gathered. *If I run there, I can grab that piece before the heat gets too unbearable*, he thought to himself. *Or, send someone to grab it.*

"I need a volunteer. And someone to build a research hut for me," the Elf called out to the crowd. "I must be able to study this object to know what it is and why several fell from the heavens this night." The crowd murmured. Why would anyone help some crusty old hermit who never talked with them before? Who did he think he was, wanting this help from *them*.

"I can help," another Elf said, stepping out of the crowd. "What do you need me to do?"

The hermit handed his spyglass to the volunteer and directed him to where the piece of the orb had landed. After describing what he needed, his volunteer Elf ran out to retrieve the chunk. He used his hands to test the heat of the fragment before picking it up. *Smarter than I expected.* The Elf helper ran back with the object and handed it to the hermit, who was nearly bouncing with glee. This could advance his research of the night sky by decades. Now he just had to figure out what this thing actually was. To do that he would need his observatory, or at least a building and his tools. And peace and quiet.

"Come with me. You will help me figure out what this thing is," the hermit said to his volunteer. "The rest of you, watch the orb, but do *not* attempt to disturb it, or me. I must determine what this thing is." And with that, the crowd turned back to the orb and ignored the hermit, who was already making his way back to his observatory. Or at least, what was left of it.

Chapter Three

Despite being small enough to carry in both hands, the fragment of the orb was still quite heavy. The hermit had to stop a few times during the mile journey back to the observatory to set it down and stretch his fingers. The edges were smooth and rounded, making it easy enough to carry, but the weight was still astounding. The piece of whatever it happened to be felt like a large gemstone. In fact, it was polished much like a fine topaz; sunlight glinted from the surface, held just so the dazzling blue made it difficult to look at directly. Even in the shade it was still quite bright. This puzzled the hermit, and his volunteer, more.

The falling object had ruined the observatory and the telescope was peeking through the rubble of what had once been the roof. Blessedly, the laboratory was relatively undamaged. There, the hermit was able to get a closer look at the object, inspecting it thoroughly. He documented everything he found; anything could be useful with this object. He used several tools, all of which he had made himself, to test the strength and toughness of the fragment. The volunteer, the hermit hadn't asked his name, looked at everything in the laboratory, attempted to determine what everything was and what it all did. He was a curious, helpful Elf. That alone was more than could be said of many others.

"I believed this object was simply reflecting the light from the sun, but it continues to emit its own light. This is quite...*curious* don't you think?" the hermit asked, hoping the volunteer knew he was being talked to.

"I agree. What causes the light?"

An inquisitive mind, I see. That is handy. "You ask many intriguing questions, volunteer," the hermit replied.

"Call me Kieran, if you wish," he answered.

"Very well, Kieran." The hermit put down the tool he had been using and went to a wall to grab another tool hanging there. He needed something to help him see *into* the object. Something was inside it, and he wanted to see. "My name is Fylson, though most simply call me *the hermit* because I like being alone."

"People attempt to label what they don't understand. It is a desire to feel comforted and superior, Fylson," Kieran replied, examining a map of the night sky that hung on one of the walls. "This map is fascinating."

"I spent the past four years carefully documenting the sky to make that. Please do not touch it; the parchment is quite fragile."

Fylson continued working on the fragment of the orb until the moon rose above the horizon to the south and east, as the map depicted. Something about the object seemed familiar. Known to him. He could not place why.

Chapter Four

It's a *star!* A star that *fell* from the heavens!" Fylson shouted, examining the star fragment under a magnifying lens.

"Are you sure? How can we verify this?" Kieran asked.

"Why did they fall? Can we use them? If we can use them, is the remainder of the star going to offer more use to us?" Fylson countered.

The pair stared at the star fragment for several minutes, attempting to learn what they could from it. Nothing about it seemed abnormal, besides that it emitted its own light. The color had changed slightly, from a bright topaz to a brilliant sapphire, a deep blue in color. Something caused this change, but what? It had also cooled significantly, no longer retaining any warmth. *Perhaps that caused the change in the color?* Fylson took notes of this observation, to compare with the larger portion of the star later.

As Fylson and Kieran continued to examine the star fragment, the shell surrounding the internal light cracked and startled the two who stepped back immediately. The crack spread and within moments had completely broken open as simply as a chicken egg. Fylson approached and reached out to touch the shell, ever so gently putting pressure on the surface. The entire fragment dissolved into a sludge that climbed onto the hermit's hand and covered his skin in a faint blue film.

Chapter Five

Master Fylson are you hurt?" Kieran asked, as he tried to find something to gather the film into and at least get it off the hermit.

"It doesn't hurt! I actually feel...powerful. I don't know how to exactly describe the feeling. It's *wonderful*."

The film had now covered Fylson from head to toe, the blue tint fading as it spread across his body. Even the film itself faded, absorbing into his skin, like a clear lacquer spread on a wooden door. Suddenly his body jolted, his muscles stiffened instantly, then contracted a moment later. Fylson shouted in agony and dropped to his knees, visibly weak from the struggle with the foreign film that had dissolved into his body. A few minutes later, he was able to stand, supporting himself with the edge of the table.

"I need to rest. I have been up for nearly three days, examining the star, which has suddenly disappeared and taken me as a *host*. I just need rest," Fylson said, briefly letting go of the table, then dropping to his knees.

Kieran stood nearby, unsure what to do. He dared not touch Fylson for fear of the film transferring to him. The convulsions looked unpleasant and if he could, he would rather avoid that. Kieran left the room and returned a moment later with a small wooden bowl filled with warm water and a pinch of tea leaves. Tendrils of steam rose from the water which Kieran had put over the hearth earlier that day. Fylson drank the tea before it could fully steep and left only a few leaf specks in the bowl. He seemed to regain some strength from the drink, and stood on his own, wobbling only momentarily.

"I will sleep. You should return home and come back in the morning. I suspect we will have much studying ahead of us." Fylson said, walking toward the spiraling stairs leading down to his chambers.

Up the stairs, the telescope peeked through the rubble that had once been the observatory. Kieran stayed behind a moment, watching Fylson to make sure he was still fine. The hermit turned and saw his volunteer still standing at the table, the empty wooden bowl still in his hands. Fylson felt an anger growing inside him, unusual for him, seeing the Elf ignoring something he had said. He raised his left hand toward the Elf before speaking again.

"Go home and rest!"

A small beam of blue light jumped from Fylson and slammed into Kieran then absorbed into him just as it had with Fylson. Both Elves stopped where they were and shared a look of disbelief. *What just happened?* Fylson saw the same expression of Kieran's face as he knew to be on his own. Curious, Fylson looked to a candle on a nearby desk and reached his hand out to it, bidding it to light. His hand tingled, and a small, jumpy flame sparked to life atop the candle, flickering on the wick like any regular flame.

Chapter Six

You just lit the candle without touching it! And you gave me the blue film," Kieran exclaimed, then protested, clearly upset about the transmission.

"Try to put out the candle. I want to see if it was an accident or if it was whatever has happened to us," Fylson replied.

Kieran reached out his hand and commanded the fire on the candle to extinguish. Both Elves gasped. Fylson, again curious tried lighting the candle without saying anything, and to his astonishment, a flame appeared atop the candle. He commanded it away, and the fire obeyed his orders, as if an invisible servant stood by the candle, obeying every command, no matter the ridiculous nature of the commander.

Kieran, without reaching out his hand and without speaking, extinguished the flame, and both Elves began rejoicing in their discovery. *I've just advanced my research by decades if not further!* Fylson quickly jotted down notes, ensuring that he captured everything about this discovery. This discovery could advance society centuries. Or annihilate it. *What a quandary.*

"What should we call this discovery?" Kieran asked, still quivering from excitement.

"Magic," Fylson replied confidently after several moments of pondering.

The Collapse of Madira

Chapter One

ive hundred and two years into the First Era, the sun rose over the world, casting light across the surface of the planet. No one in the mine could see the sun, but the Dwarves preferred life that way. It was a vast, deep, and intricate mine, about three kilometers down from the original entrance near the peak of the mountain. The mine consisted of a shaft about a kilometer wide, with a road that spiraled down to the deepest levels. The road itself was wide enough for two horse-drawn wagons to pass each other. Every fifty kilometers going into the mine, there was a level with branch shooting off from the main shaft. One level had a north and south branch, the next level had east and west branches. About six levels below ground level, roughly three hundred meters, there were two additional mine shafts with smaller spiraling roads. The additional shafts were a kilometer east and west from the main mine shaft. The branch mines between the original entrance and the new ground-level entrances had been converted into homes for the miners, smiths, and their families. All life revolved around the mines of Madira.

The mine had a sharp, hot smell, especially deeper in the mine, since there was, at the deepest part of the main shaft, a pool of exposed magma. The Dwarves used the magma to heat their furnaces that smelted the ore gathered from elsewhere in the mine. Specially made carts were used to bring magma up to the furnaces and forges. After smelting and refining the ore, the dwarves sold the metal to various cities and blacksmiths across Drendil. Everything and everyone had and knew their place. The system worked well.

A series of bells, placed throughout the mine, rang out, marking the sixth hour. Madira, the Dwarven Capital mine, ran deep. The mine had originally started near the top of a mountain and was built into the icy cliffs stretching for kilometers above. The Dwarves added another entrance about a century before, closer to the base of the mountain. Most merchant wagons came in, or out, of the mine through that newer entrance, a long tunnel that ran through the mountain.

The only hint that the sun had risen, apart from the bells' pealing, was the clanging of hammers and picks, the barking of orders, and the singing of songs. Despite what surface-dwellers thought, the Dwarves were a happy people. Sanwada Hillhide, the

Dwarven Queen, kept her people happy and wealthy. Endless supplies of metals and precious gemstones flowed out of the mine, which kept the coffers full. Only during a couple of years, near the start of their mining, had there been shortages of food.

Queen Sanwada was tall for the Dwarven people; she stood over a meter and a half, even though she was about eighty years old, and since the typical lifespan for a Dwarf was one hundred and twenty years she was still fairly young. Her hair was golden-red with white scattered throughout, about the color of a polished citrine. Her bright green eyes shone brilliantly and stood out from her heart-shaped face with high cheekbones, a long, slender nose, and a smile as warm as a hundred sunsets. Even with her uncanny ability to make pleasantries, she also had a temper that could break a mountain! She learned to be slow to anger. This was no easy feat. And little would help anyone who faced her temper

Bammog Goldbreaker, a dwarf known throughout the mines, wiped the sweat from his brow with a heavy leather glove-clad hand. The dark leather glove glistened as the sweat trickled down the back of his hand. Callouses under the glove throbbed under the weight of the new pickaxe. He loved getting a new pickaxe until his hands ached. A new pickaxe meant he could mine better which meant he got paid more. *Silly surface sods*, Bammog thought to himself. *Paying shitloads for shiny stones when they could do the work themselves.*

Bammog had been the only child in his family. But due to tragedy, he became an orphan early in his life. He was stout and barrel-chested standing shorter than his Queen, an average height for a Dwarf. He was in his late 30s, still a young dwarf. He had chocolate brown hair, thick eyebrows, broad shoulders with thick arms. He had a bulbous nose, green eyes, and a rough complexion, developed from the twelve years spent mining. He had a distinguishable round face, low cheekbones, a rough smile, and a missing tooth, right in the front of his mouth, hard to miss once.

Bammog had an easy-going temperament, which was in direct contrast to the nickname he had been given by the other Dwarves. They called him "Ox." Nevertheless, Bammog enjoyed his work, extremely hardworking, often happy to work, and would rarely stop until he physically couldn't mine anymore. Hiding his powerful jaw was a thick, short beard, almost black. And like many of the hardworking dwarf mineworkers, he had rough, calloused hands, and dry, sandpapery elbows.

The Elves saw the Dwarves as little more than a free people of slaves. Slaves to the market, to money, living beneath the world's tough skin. Slaves living among stone. *But the Elves are only happy with their magic, reading their fancy books and scrolls.* At least that's how the tales spoke. Few Dwarves *wanted* to see the surface world, and even fewer made it through the gates.

Bammog let the thoughts of the surface world carry him away. He could not help but laugh to himself about the silly Elves living in their towers, gazing longingly at their precious stars. *The fools.* Bammog continued to swing his pickaxe, looking for that special glint that told him something valuable was hidden within the thick stone, hidden from the world. Many secrets remained to be uncovered in the tough stone.

His father, Hoful, had been a stout man but less muscular than his son Bammog. He would have been in his early seventies, were he still alive. Tragically, he was killed when one of the branch mines collapsed when Bammog was ten years old. His father's father was Bhastec who had been the youngest of six children. He was a strong man who worked in the mines for sixty years. He was short and hunched over from age. His entire life had revolved around the mines. He even used his old pickaxe as a walking cane. Bhastec had had wispy, white hair with a thinning, long beard that came to his waist. He had a large, beak of a nose. Bhastec had died in his sleep a year before.

Hoful and Bhastec, and now Bammog, had made their living finding gold or jewels that got carted off to the surface dwellers. Bammog's family had fed the surface world's entire, precious economy. He had not earned the right to rest yet so there he stood, swinging his pickaxe, mining for gemstones. Emeralds were common finds. They were a dazzling green, easy to see among the browns and greys of the stone.

Flakes of stone that chipped away with each swing of the pickaxe turned into sharp chunks as the Dwarf strengthened his blows. Bammog continued wiping sweat from his thick brow. Small glimmers of tiny gem flakes glistened on the floor, enough to pay for food that day. But Bammog wanted a bath. *A* warm *bath*, he reminded himself. Cold water was nice, but it had been a week since his last hot bath. Firewood was a commodity for the Dwarves. *Funny*, Bammog thought to himself, *how we rely on the surface world to provide wood for our fires, and they rely on us to provide the shiny stones they crave so badly.* He could use oil to warm his bathwater, but he had to choose between that or his food. A tough choice, but one that sometimes had to be made.

Chapter Two

After another few hours, Bammog started swinging his pickaxe vigorously. *A vein! I found a vein!* Emerald chips glinted through the air as they tumbled to the floor. This vein was longer than his arm, and bigger around than his waist. He could get an assignment to a different mine with this haul! He kept picking away, chipping more stone away from the vein with each swing. As the chips flew dramatically, it revealed more of the faint, glinting emerald through the stone. As Bammog continued swinging his pickaxe, the vein was revealed to be even longer, going deeper into the stone than he was tall. This piece of emerald alone had to weigh over one hundred pounds! It would be easier to carry it from the mine to the foreman in pieces, he thought. Switching gears, Bammog began swinging his pickaxe at the emerald to break off a sizable chunk, which fell to the ground with a heavy *thud*.

Grabbing the large chunk of unpolished emerald, Bammog hefted it over his shoulder and carried it back up the tunnel toward the foreman, who inspected all the gems and minerals workers excavated from the mines. Upon seeing Bammog with the large piece of emerald, the foreman's eyes widened, and his jaw dropped. Had it been a leg of mutton, he would have been drooling on his foot.

"Bam, ya bastard, what is that on your shoulder?! Where did you get that?" the foreman said, bringing attention from other workers nearby. They were now rushing to see one of the biggest pieces of emerald found in the mine for years! So many miners could live comfortably from even a fist-sized piece of emerald.

"I found a vein. Believe if you want, but this is a small piece," Bammog replied. Some miners ran down the tunnel upon hearing about an emerald vein.

Already, a swarm of miners had gathered, wanting, longing to see the emerald vein that started at half the size of Bam to so big it could block the doors at the top of the mine as it was told from row to row. Word had spread four levels up and three down, amusement buzzing through the mine. Another dwarf returned with another large lump of emerald from the vein, about half the size of what Bammog had broken from the wall.

"Hey, put that back! This is Bam's find. He gets the money for this one. You know better, Lof," the foreman called. "And don't you give any lip. I don't care how much is there, it's his."

Bammog set the emerald down on the scale and, as he suspected, it was just shy of one hundred pounds. *Gods, the pay for this will be huge.* The foreman wrote down the weight, hefted the chunk into a minecart, then motioned for Bammog to go back to get the rest of the vein. He was only supposed to be in the mine for a couple more hours before getting some food; it shouldn't take more than that to get the rest of the vein. *At least the biggest pieces,* Bammog told himself. Once again, he lifted the pickaxe, feeling warmth in his callouses. Maybe he would have a blister the next day. But he could stop mining for a month at this point. Why worry about blisters now? It seemed pointless to worry about that when he would be relaxing in a warm bathtub tonight.

Ting. Ting. Ting. The steel of the pickaxe rang out against the hard stone as he worked at freeing the rest of the vein. Time passed; the floor became littered with stone. Bammog freed another section of the vein from the stone, another hundred-pound behemoth, even minus the piece that Lof had chipped out. *Where did that end up?* Bammog shrugged and went back to mining. He heaved the pickaxe over his shoulder, arced it forward, then dropped it against the exposed emerald. As the pickaxe made contact, the gem split, and a light brighter than all the torches in the mine combined started pouring out. Liquid light. It melted the emerald as it dripped down to the floor; the pickaxe had already melted away; the haft now was no more than a torch. Bammog dropped the haft of his former pickaxe and tripped as he stepped backward, shrieked, and covered his eyes from the blinding light. The light kept pouring from the emerald, now gushing forth in more places as the light started melting away more of the gem.

Chapter Three

Rendil was a relatively new continent with three main races: Elves, humans, and Dwarves. The Elves and humans shared a joint, dual-ruler kingdom that had mostly been peaceful. Unfortunately, after the Elves discovered Magic, others started practicing Dark Magic, and their experiments created monsters, and Madness. It was a disease that spread through the Dark Magic users, who were driven insane and started wars. One war took place after the Elves banned the humans from the sorcerers' college, thinking the humans had been the cause of the Dark Magic, after an incident at the College.

The Dwarves, after discovering gold, silver, gems, and other precious metals, receded into the mountains, cutting themselves off from the surface world. The Dwarves haven't dealt with Magic, Dark Magic, Madness, or any of the other problems the surface world has faced in the centuries since the Dwarves had formed their metallurgic practices.

The northern lands were cold and icy, but in the middle and southern parts of the continent, it grew more temperate with some dry areas to the west of the mountains where Madira and the other Dwarven mines were found. The continent's overall population was small, roughly twenty million on the surface, spread throughout the continent. For the Dwarves, their population, split between the three cities, numbered roughly six million total Dwarves, with Madira being the largest of the mines.

A small cart, pulled by a stubborn, aged donkey, rolled down a packed dirt road heading toward Madira. The wheels creaking as they rolled along the rough dirt. The driver of the cart carried a small whip to get the donkey moving but rarely had to use it, as the animal had grown used to the route into the mountains. The road rose gently in the forest near the mountains, then raised aggressively as the hills suddenly became mountains. Birds fluttered through the trees and sang their songs, accompanying the merchant along his ride. The smell of fresh earth in the forest was strong, and the ground glistened from the recent rainfall. Enough rain for everything to stay green, but not enough to leave the road a muddy mess. The merchant looked up, letting the donkey drive the wagon on its own, as he watched the fluffy white clouds descend from the mountains—

The mountain with the entrance to Madira suddenly *splashed* into a burst of light as bright as the sun with the ground peeling up before it collapsed. The ground vibrated, warped, and cracked beneath the cart. The donkey, spooked by the commotion, started running, the only direction it knew was toward the growing ball of light coming from what used to be Madira. Suddenly the whole area collapsed into the former mine, sending the wagon, merchant, and donkey plummeting into an immense hole. Something struck the merchant in the back of the head and suddenly everything went dark. The last thing he heard was the donkey braying, then a wet *squish*.

Chapter Four

The day had been quiet thus far. As a Dwarven Councilor, there was very little that happened in the mountains that needed to be reported to others. Unfortunately, the quiet day quickly came to an end when the light appeared and the mountains that had formerly been Madira had collapsed. It changed the landscape greatly.

Reidoul Oakenaxe worked at his small stone desk with wooden legs. The desk would have been small for a human, but for a Dwarf, it was large and luxurious. His office was a bit peculiar by human standards because it was inside a tunnel in a mountain. No window marred the stone walls around him because there was nothing worth seeing! His shelves were cluttered with books, scrolls, maps, and many other miscellaneous objects befitting a Councilor. Within the office were also numerous logs of the shipments of everything that came in and out of the mountains. In addition to being a Councilor, he was the Scout Commander for the Dwarven kingdom of Madira. And like every day, today was no different. There he sat, reading through the reports from all of the scouts, again.

The entire mountain had collapsed into light. Reidoul could only wonder how something like that even happens. A mountain had collapsed a few hundred years ago when a star had fallen out of the sky and crashed into the mountain range. An Elf had been the one to determine they were stars, right before discovering magic from the core of a star.

Reidoul sat at his heavy stone desk which was made from the very stone that had once formed the tunnel his office sat in. A knock sounded at the door, but before Reidoul could get up to answer the door, an Elf entered the room. He wore a dark robe with a cowl covering his long, blonde hair, pulled back from his face with a string. His hands were in the sleeves of his robe, concealing his long, thin fingers. The Elf could not stand at his full height until he was in the room, ducking through the door. Once in the room, he removed his cowl, revealing pointed ears, one of the few features common between the Dwarven and Elven peoples. His eyes, green like a forest covering the foothills of a mountain, shone in the lamplight. He stood thin and lanky, with broad shoulders, an unbelievably sinewy build. Reidoul noticed that he had a very strong jawline and he looked young for an Elf, but there was little way of knowing his age.

"How can I help you, Master Elf?" Reidoul asked, not standing from his desk. It was *his* office after all. He didn't have to stand for *anyone* other than the Queen, who had been missing since the mine collapsed.

"I am here to discuss today's events. We sensed danger and began watching the source with our magic. It's a complicated process I don't wish to explain, not that you would understand it," the Elf began, not giving his name. It seemed intentional.

"What could you possibly know about the collapse?" asked Reidoul with a sense of urgency and suspicion.

"The accident was caused when a dwarf, one Bammog Goldbreaker, found what he thought was an emerald vein. This is somewhat true; however, beneath the vein was the core of a star that fell several hundred years ago. When he struck the core, the outer wall split, emitting the same light that provides the source of all magic. With nowhere to go, the light caused an eruption which began eating through the stone. This eruption caused the collapse as there was soon no support for the mine, which weakened the mountain. Have you surveyed the extent of the collapse?" The Elf asked, showed no emotion. He might as well have been reading off an order of roasted leg of lamb, potatoes, and mixed vegetables from a menu.

"We haven't had a chance to get close enough. The mine has been too hot to get within the better part of a kilometer without getting burned. Since ye know so much, when should we be able to get to the mine? Have you seen our Queen through your fancy magic things that I won't understand?" pressed the Elf. Reidoul made his dislike of the Elf as clear as he could without changing his face or tone.

"We have not seen your Queen, but if she was in the mine…" The Elf dared not finish the sentence for fear of being thrown through the door. He continued, choosing his words cautiously. "In about a week or so the heat should reduce enough to, at the very least, survey the damage from the surface. Likely, very little of the mine will be salvageable. Do you have any other questions?"

"Had the star core not been discovered at the end of a pickaxe, what could the Dwarf society have become?" Reidoul only asked out of pure curiosity.

"Do you want an answer to that question?"

"No. Dwelling on the possibilities will change naught about the situation"

"Then I shall take my leave," the Elf responded, donning his cowl before leaving the room. Once the door closed, Reidoul heard a faint *fhisk* sound and saw some light shining under the door. And with that, the Elf was gone and Reidoul was left pondering what had happened, how it had happened, and most of all: Why? What was the reason that today happened the way it had happened? *Suppose that question may never be answered. Unless you're an Elf.*

Chapter Five

Just as the Elf had said, the mine, or rather the hole where the mine had been, took a few days past a week to cool down enough to survey the damage done during the collapse. Unfortunately, from what Reidoul was seeing, no one would have survived either the collapse itself or the time after the star meltdown. Not even charred remains littered the mine. Hundreds of thousands of Dwarves had been in the mine that day, and thousands were presumed dead. With little else to go by, the Dwarves assumed their fearless leader, Queen Sanwada, the first Queen of Madira, perished during the collapse of the biggest mine in the kingdom. Vilyar would now be the capital mine, with its ample supply of gold and silver veins. It was a smaller mine, but it would bring the most money for the kingdom.

Reidoul swore, seeing the damage done. Entire pathways had been melted by the light. The stone previously blasted with explosives was now nowhere to be found. The entire mountain had collapsed into a crater. No visible, safe path existed to get further into the mine than the surface. And even then, the heat was coming from the deepest parts of the former mine, radiating toward the sky. Birds circled overhead, rising high above the pit without having to flap their wings.

Nothing left to salvage from the mine. No Queen to lead the kingdom. *Much* less source of money and supplies. The Dwarven Kingdom would surely face a collapse as epic as this mine. *Shame.* Reidoul made the journey back to his office to write a report to send to Vilyar with his recommendations. The other Councilors would have to make their decision based on his report. Nothing. That was his recommendation. Nothing. Nothing could be done. Nothing could be saved. Nothing exists of the mine or the mountain. Nothing.

Dark Magic

Chapter One

Water slowly dripped from the rough, stone ceiling, and added to the moist mustiness of the dungeon. The entire place smelled of stagnant water as if a heavy rain flooded the dungeon years ago and it never dried out. A draft trickled in from somewhere, which was odd since the entire facility was underground. None of the cells would have been considered inviting to anything other than insects, but what good was an inviting dungeon? The College diligently claimed to be open and accepting of all Magic users. Despite the welcoming speeches, there could be no denial that the College had, and used, dungeons for their more...*sinister* guests. On the surface, the College played their cards to be inviting, warmly accepting anyone who wanted to learn the ways of Magic; truthfully, they were not as warm and inviting as they made themselves appear. Make a small mistake and you ended up in the dungeon. The length of your stay was determined by your crime, and which of the College Councilors sentenced you.

The entire dungeon was dark, minus a small light emanating from a few candles on the rickety, pinewood table nearby and the ashen remnants of a small fire that had nearly burned out in the hearth. The cell doors were woven cast iron, reinforced with simple spells that even a small child could have cast. Due to their nature, the captive inside the cell could only sense the spells, not any further source of Magic. Even the walls reverberated with the spell. Fascinating.

A heavy *chunk* sounded from the far end of the dungeon when the key turned the lock inside the door. The latch released and the door opened. The warden, identified by his overly simple epaulets, walked down the narrow, poorly lit hallway. His heavy footsteps marked his presence only moments before the smell of cabbage and beef, which oozed from the pores of his skin. The man reeked of cabbage every time he came for one of his "visits." Perhaps he bathed in the vile vegetable. The warden was surprisingly stout and barrel-chested for an Elf—he was built very much like a tall Dwarf. He wore a uniform that barely fit him as if he put on clothes from his son's wardrobe. His buttons strained over his paunch of a belly. Stains, visible even in the poor light, had long-ago been smeared into the tan fabric of his shirt. The only thing he wore that was the proper size were his boots. They seemed to awkwardly fit his feet and glistened in the light of the torch he carried. An almost flowery smell, barely detected beneath the waves of cabbage, accompanied him. He had polished his boots earlier that day, perhaps for a visit with the Council. It was odd that his boots were the best-kept part of his uniform.

Dark curly hair prominently stood atop his head and he had one good eye. The warden was an odd man to deal with, the prisoner thought. The warden had a scar that went from the left corner of his mouth to the bottom of his left ear. The scar, however old it was, had never properly healed. It forced the wardens' mouth into an almost permanent, lopsided smile. His dark green eyes were narrow and made him look like he was constantly squinting. Bushy eyebrows, which had never been trimmed in his life, nearly touched above his eyes. They resembled two caterpillars that perched themselves at the bottom of his brow. His jagged nose was crooked, pointing severely to the left as if he had caught a few too many fists with his face over the years of overseeing the College's dungeon.

The warden's visits had always been severely…inquisitive and rougher than they needed to be, probing into the practices which led to the dungeon being occupied by its singular guest. The answers that were provided by the captive had not been the correct or desired answers to the questions the warden asked.

Before he reached for the door to the cell, the warden first waved his hands and silently dismissed the spells only long enough to open the door. The spells both locked the doors and locked out Magic for anyone inside the cell. One of the guards who accompanied the warden was an oafish Elf wearing chainmail armor under a woolen tabard with a dark leather belt and a cudgel on his left hip. With a wave of his gloved hand, the guard recast the spell. In that brief moment, the captive reached out, searching for the sweet, life-giving connection to the Magic he so desired. The connection that he had so forcefully been removed from. The fount of life-giving Magic was just beyond reach. That was the most frustrating part about being in the dungeon. He couldn't touch that power he craved. Once the door closed, the spell reengaged and that distant power once more vanished, the spell being the only remotely tangible Magic.

Inside the cell, the warden, like his captive, was disconnected from Magic. The warden *was* just an Elf, and the captive knew he could easily overpower the fat sack of cabbage even without his Magic. It was the other guards that would provide some difficulty fighting. They still had their Magic. There had to be a way to use the barrier spells against the warden. There just had to be.

"Are we ready to talk yet?" the warden inquired with his thickly accented dialect that dripped with hints of having lived in the highlands of Drendil. This was a distinctly local voice that was shared by many of the Elves. He reeked of the Highlands and cabbage. It was a rancid combination.

"What would you like to talk about?" the captive asked, though he knew exactly how the warden would respond to the question.

"The rituals. The same thing I've wanted to know about this whole time," the warden barked, his voice echoing off the stone walls.

Right on cue, the captive thought to himself. "I can't talk about the specifics of them. I told you that."

"You're going to talk about them," the warden stated, his voice flat.

"You haven't listened to anything I have told you already. Have I refused to tell you about the rituals?" the captive asked.

The warden was silent for several moments, contemplating what had been said. He finally agreed that, no, the captive had not been refusing to talk.

"I have not refused to answer. I have said I *cannot* talk about the rituals, not that I *will* not. There are spells in place that prevent anyone involved from speaking about the rituals. You can attempt to remove the spells if you would like, but you'll need to touch the Dark Magic that you so strongly dread. And to do that, you need me to be in a room where both of us can use Magic, and we both know that isn't going to happen. Am I right about that, warden?"

"You are right about that. So, there are silencing spells that keep you from talking about the rituals? Why go through so much trouble if you claim that what you are practicing shouldn't be feared?" the warden asked, pausing again. "If you can't speak about the rituals, can you speak to who is involved? Or where you meet for these rituals?"

"Let's find out what the bond allows me to mention."

Chapter Two

...Two months earlier...

The dim cave was cool, damp, and musty, much as a cave should be. White minerals formed stalactites that descended from the ceiling high above, decorating the cave with stone teeth. Similarly, stalagmites rose from the cave floor, some meeting their ceiling-bound brothers, others simply climbing toward the cavern's roof. Lamps and candles, scattered around the cave, cast shadows on the rocky formations. The shadows danced with the flames. The sound of water dripping from the ceiling echoed through the cave. *Drip. Drip. Drip.*

Within the cave, about a dozen men and Elves gathered. Each wore black robes, their faces covered by deep cowls. Everyone kept their eyes cast toward the ground, watching only where they walked or stood. Those gathered formed a ring around a marking that was etched into the floor of the cave. The marking showed a hexagon bound by a circle. The points of the star reached beyond the edge of the circle. Symbols from the old Elven Tongue were etched in the stone around the points of the star, one on each side of the point, and another aligned with the points themselves. The marking glowed a deep purple. The light throbbed incessantly as everyone gathered around it.

One of the tall and lean Elves, with fine sandy hair falling from the front of his cowl, began chanting words from his ancient tongue. The marking on the floor changed colors and ceased to throb. The marking turned red and shone bright and steady. The others around the circle joined in the chant, their voices drowning out the dripping of the water elsewhere in the cave.

During the chanting, a doorway made of light and darkness opened in the air over the markings; the opening in the air shimmered and its edges distorted anything seen through them, much like the air that wriggled over a fire. Had anyone touched the doorway, the edges would have been icy cold as it was made of Magic and connected to a world far beyond this one. A distorted face appeared in the doorway, looking upon those gathered; judging their worthiness; deciding if the participants were worthy of its time.

"Who has summoned me?" the face said. Its deep voice was almost a growl. The voice filled the cave and echoed off the stone interior.

"I, Kel'ren, of the Assembly of Mages have summoned you, Great One," the Elf said, bowing deeply from the waist.

"Why have you summoned me?"

"Great One, we seek knowledge and power that mortals in this plane do not grant. We humbly beseech you—" Kel'ren said, before getting cut off by the mysterious face.

"None of you are powerful enough to be sorcerers. You are children claiming titles you have not earned. You do not warrant my attention, mortal. None before me are strong enough to touch my power. Return when you have the necessary strength."

With that, the face and the doorway where it appeared, vanished as if neither had ever been there. The markings on the wall returned to their original color. The light once again began throbbing. The group stood there, downtrodden by the news they had received.

Chapter Three

Was this the only ritual? You, being human, are not Kel'ren, if that is even his real name. Do you know the names of any others attending this ritual?" the warden asked, leaning against the wall of the cell.

"There were other rituals. That was the only one with the portal and face."

"What can you tell me about this Assembly of Mages?" the warden unceasingly inquired.

"They are the ones who started the rituals. No one among the group uses names other than Kel'ren. Since we always wear hoods, I've never seen the others' faces," the captive responded.

"So clearly none of you wish to be known," the warden surmised. "What is the purpose of the Assembly of Mages? What do they do?"

"They organize the rituals and attempt to gain knowledge and powers from another plane. We believe there is more to Magic to be discovered beyond our world, and clearly, the face told us we aren't strong enough." The captive continued, "The College is failing all who come here, teaching limited spells, letting students only touch a portion of the pool of Magic." The warden asked, "So, you wish to bring down the College?"

"Not at all," responded the captive. "We simply think the College and students would benefit from learning all there is to discover about Magic. And there is power waiting for us beyond this realm. We simply need to learn what is needed to gain that power."

"What has the Assembly done to gain this sought-after power?" The warden asked, picking his questions more carefully.

"There is only so much I can tell you with this bond. Remove it and I can tell you more than you want to know about the Assembly," the captive replied.

Chapter Four

…Six Weeks Earlier…

If the moon was in the sky, it could not be seen. Clouds formed high overhead and covered the sky, as far as could be seen. The Assembly of Mages gathered in a dense forest. They never met in the same place twice in a row, to avoid detection. Their activities, while not menacing on their own, would be seen as expellable offenses by the College.

The forest was composed of densely clustered oak and maple trees, things that could withstand most of the weather throughout the year. It never got cold enough for the leaves to fall from the trees. The Assembly gathered in a small clearing around a boulder that was partially freed from the ground. The boulder showed the same markings as those in the cave. The markings were only visible after the proper spell had been cast against the tough stone. This collection of symbols glowed green, but once again the light pulsed as the Assembly gathered. Supposedly, this location and markings would open a different portal. They were calling a different being in what they speculated was a different plane of existence. Perhaps this being would be more charitable with its powers. The Assembly had neither learned the names of these Great Ones they contacted, nor had they assigned any names to them for fear of offending the beings with the wrong name.

This meeting followed the same process as before. Kel'ren began the chanting, the markings changed colors, and the rest of the group joined in. Spells cast by multiple mages working together were always stronger. It also allowed one mage to cast an infinitely stronger spell without becoming exhausted so quickly. Another portal opened this time. This portal was more oval-shaped than the previous one, but with the same illusion of fire around the edges. Another face appeared in this portal, demanding the chanting to stop.

"Why have you summoned me?"

"Great One, grant us your powers," Kel'ren said, not identifying himself this time.

"Who are you to command me, mortal? the being asked with a booming voice."

"I bring you a sacrifice," he replied, waving his right hand toward a bound Elf who had accompanied the Assembly.

"This pleases me. Bring him forward," the Great One replied.

The Elf was brought to the portal. The Great One's face grew larger within the mirror-like surface, examining the Elf closely. The Elf trembled and his ears quivered. The Great One continued to examine the Elf, starting at the top of his head, looking closely at his hair, both in color and quality. His gaze moved down, examining his muscular structure, the shape of his body, the length of his arms and fingers, everything. Finally, the Great One moved back, returning to his original location within the portal.

"This host pleases me," the Great One said, immediately flashing from the portal into the Elf's mouth, turning into the light as he splashed from the portal.

The sacrifice fell to the ground and his body convulsed momentarily before he finally stood up. The Great One, now within the body of the Elf, looked at the bindings and wiggled his fingers. The ropes flashed in flame, like the wick of a candle. Within an instant, the ropes were gone, but the skin remained unscathed.

"I will grant you my powers," the Great one said.

The moment he ended his decree, a dark, billowing illumination emerged from the Elf who now hosted the Great One. The light covered the Assembly and their bodies absorbed the dark aura quickly. Within moments, the event was finished and the Great One flashed from his host back into the portal. The sacrificial Elf's body went limp and fell to the ground where it remained motionless. The portal closed and everything went back to how it had been a few short moments before. Insects chirped and buzzed in the trees, an owl hooted in the distance, and the dark clouds overhead still blocked any light from the moon.

Chapter Five

You sacrificed an Elf to this being!" The warden protested after the recollection of the event.

"I am telling you what I can tell you. The Elf volunteered to be the sacrifice, but he hadn't been told everything that would happen. Still, he volunteered," the captive responded.

"The Council will need to hear about this," the warden said, standing from his spot on the wall.

The oafish guard outside of the cell undid the spell on the door, and the captive reached out to the Magic he craved. He touched that fount of power for a moment, then the spell re-engaged. So close. The spell on the door, the only Magic the captive could sense, was weaker than before. *Curious*, he thought to himself.

"Keep that human where he is, and don't lower the spells until I return," the warden ordered before his heavy footsteps accompanied him down the hall, marking his departure.

The heavy *chunk* at the end of the hall marked the opening of the door and the hinges squeaked from their lack of grease. The guards never returned to stand outside the door, as they did before. Something was different now. The spell was still on the door, but it felt weaker, less present than before. Something was happening, and the prisoner was curious- though he would not bring up the weakness of the spell; that could change these new dynamics. Perhaps, the Assembly had someone inside the dungeon who was trying to get him free? *Only time will tell on that one*, the prisoner thought to himself.

Chapter Six

...A Month Before...

The past two weeks were filled with experiments and testing, conducted as secretly as was feasible, within the Sorcerer's College. So many powers had been discovered. things were very different at the College. Fire spells that burned hotter than anything they had learned to cast from the College. Lightning sprouted from their hands, even summoning specters, that, though they posed no threat and could harm nothing, had been armed with weapons. These specters appeared to be warriors from the past. Perhaps, the poor wretches were the souls of soldiers from the Mages' War from so many years ago. Their souls never found the peace that would let them leave the spirit world. The next test with the specters would be to determine if the weapons could harm anything in this realm. If they couldn't harm anything, there hardly seemed a reason to summon the specters in the future.

Spells were stronger and seemed less intensive to cast, fatiguing the wizards less than standard Magic learned from the College. This would be something the College would not want known. Stronger spells and less fatigue would make the wizards, sorcerers, mages, and anyone else casting spells nearly unstoppable. Especially since the destructive spells were more efficient. They had discovered a fire spell that spouted as a liquid before engulfing various testing targets in flames. These spells produced flames that spread more fiercely than had been seen before. Luckily, the stones that made up the buildings were imbued with Magic to absorb spells and prevent destructive spells from spreading. Otherwise, the entire College could have burned down after one of the Elves had 'accidentally' tried the wrong fire spell after one of their classes.

Long after the sun descended beyond the western horizon the Assembly gathered in the same forest where the powers had been granted to them. On the stone marking laid two more sacrifices, bound with spells to prevent them from shouting. The sacrifices waited impatiently on the boulder for another experiment. Twenty new Mages joined the Assembly, and now all would pool their strengths. The brigade was led by Kel'ren, to see what powers could be gained by having multiple casters throwing the same spell. This wouldn't be a destructive spell, but one that was, according to Kel'ren, supposed to alter the volunteers' bodies. What the alteration was supposed to do had not been disclosed to the group; discretion was important to the integrity of the Assembly. Or so they had been told by Kel'ren. Some of the Mages in the Assembly had begun to distrust Kel'ren.

The ritual started, and the group of wizards joined their powers together with Kel'ren, who was in control of the casting. He spawned a complicated spell that took his entire concentration to master. How he learned the spell was a mystery to the rest of the Assembly. The spell swirled overhead and became a tumultuous cyclone that tightened into two small orbs. One orb hovered over each of the bound sacrifices. One of the volunteers glistened from sweat collecting on her brow, neck, and between her breasts. The other, his eyes closed, had not seen the spell and was unaware of what had been happening. He trembled under his bindings.

The orbs slowly absorbed into the two sacrifices and their bodies stiffened and contorted; color rushed to their skin, which seemed to boil, something under their skin fighting for an escape. Muscles changed as well, some growing others shrinking. Skeletal structures changed to match the changing muscle groups. The bodies twisted and turned, as the Elves fought to maintain their forms. The woman, though she was bound, still screamed, a shrill, though muffled, shriek that would have echoed through the dense forest. The man moaned softly as his body stopped convulsing and slowly grew still. Within a matter of minutes, the entire affair seemed to be over.

What started as two Elves ended with two grotesque figures with some Elf qualities remaining: pointed ears, somewhat gaunt faces, sharp noses, and powerful jaws. Beyond those features, there were little similarities to the original Elves bound to the boulder. The new creatures were both squatty, slightly pot-bellied, with long arms that dangled almost to their knees, large hairy feet, and knobby knees. While the jaws were still powerful like an Elf, the underbite was extreme.

"What the hell was that experiment, Kel'ren? What have you done!" one of the mages protested, waving his hands frantically. "You said nothing about this beforehand."

"You lack the vision I have for this Assembly. Had I told anyone that we would create a new species, no one would have shown up for this ritual," Kel'ren replied calmly. "What I have done is to show us that the College is holding back their teachings. That College has the wool pulled over everyone's eyes and made us all believe we are learning the true power of Magic. They are teaching lessons for children. We have a power that they not only cannot fathom but fear without understanding why. We have created a new form of life!"

"This is wrong! What happened to these two? Did they know what would happen to them?" another mage protested, pointing at the creatures still on the rock marking.

"They knew enough of what was involved," Kel'ren defended.

"Are they still sentient beings or have you created a feral species? What of their abilities? Can they still wield Magic?" a third wizard joined the vocal protests.

"If this is what the Assembly is about, I want no part of it," another said, starting to leave. Several others had turned away from the group.

"You cannot leave! Things that take place during these rituals are far too sensitive for anyone to leave this Assembly alive," Kel'ren threatened.

"You mean to kill us for wanting nothing to do with your madness?" the future prisoner called.

"Oh, believe me, one way or another, no one will be speaking of these events," Kel'ren called, a sinister tone in his voice.

Kel'ren turned to face the protesters, casting a spell at them. The spell encircled each of those who were leaving, voicing protests. "If any of you attempt to report me to the College, you will be held prisoner and not released from the dungeon until you speak, but the bond I just placed prevents you from speaking of these events. Leave the Assembly if you wish, but you will be missing out on the powers we seek."

Chapter Seven

The door at the end of the hall opened again, announced by the creaking of its hinges. The warden had returned. He would surely be asking about the rituals again. But more importantly, he would drop the spells on the door, and the captive was already prepared for his moment. He reached. Anticipated. He wanted to touch the Magic he so desperately needed. Required. Longed for. Magic was like a long draught of water after a long day working outside in the summer, and right now, the captive was parched. His soul was parched and chapped.

The warden stopped before the door, watching the captive momentarily before he spoke, his accented voice still thick with the smell of cabbage. *Did he stop for more boiled cabbage before coming back?* The warden reeked of the bloody stuff.

"The Council wishes to speak with you, prisoner. They're on their way down here now," the warden said, as he reached out to the spell on the door. Two other guards accompanied the warden; they would have their bounds ready for the prisoner. *Why is he coming in here if the Council is coming to speak with me?*

The captive felt the spell on the door, drop. Within moments, the captive was able to contact his long-desired Magic source. His body was drenched with the power he craved. He had done it! Streams of liquid fire immediately spouted from his hands. The moment the liquid fire touched the warden's body, it melted. His flesh, even the parts that were covered in his uniform, was too soft for the liquid flames. Bolts of lightning shot towards the captive from one of the guards. The bolts zapped past the puddle that had once been the warden and struck the wall behind the prisoner. Only a few precise moves stood between the captive and his freedom. The captive reflected a new bolt of lightning toward the oaf of a guard who had launched it and watched as the fool was hurled to the far wall of the dungeon. Another stream of fire launched toward the remaining guard; the man deflected the fire into the remains of the warden; the fleshy pool boiled with the added heat. More lightning and fire were exchanged between the two for a few moments. The door at the end of the hall opened again and the creaking and heavy chunk of the latch resounded louder than the crackling of the spells. The entire dungeon smelled of ozone as the fire and lightning merged in the air. Another pair of guards rushed in, saw the captive wielding magic, and within the blink of an eye, only one guard still stood. Fire engulfed the two new arrivals.

Damn, I was so close, the captive thought to himself. Let's see if they can counter this! A stream of pure darkness, which seemed to eat the dim light around, shot forth from the cell, passing through the last guard. The shield spell he produced to protect himself did no more than paper against a rushing river. The beam of darkness wouldn't have killed the guard. All it did was push him into the wall and knock him out. But that gave more than enough time for the captive to escape, as he had intended.

All four guards lay on the ground, scattered throughout the dungeon, their bodies perfectly still. It had taken a few seconds longer than the captive originally anticipated, but he was still closer to freedom than he had been hours before. They should have had another binding spell on the outer door. The fools wanted access to their Magic, rather than keeping their prisoners castrated within the dungeon. Someone would be coming soon to investigate, for sure.

Before he could leave, the mage thought of a far-off place. Serene. Breezy. It was near the warmth of the Shimmering Ocean where a tall, stone tower stood outside the knowledge of the others. His personal space. Every Mage had their own space like his, but every mage was so different, as were their laboratories. His was a tower. Most mages only had a few rooms, except Master Fylson all those years ago. That hermit had the right idea. He had a tower and an observatory so he could watch the stars. That was how he had been able to watch the stars fall from the sky, which led to Elves and humans to find Magic. Without that discovery, society would never have reached out to worlds beyond their own.

His tower had plenty of space for experimenting and being alone. No one knew the mage's tower existed except for him since no roads led there, and he only traveled via portals.

The captive began concentrating, something he had to do more now that he was tired after the battle. Finally, after several moments of deep meditation and concentration, a portal opened in the back wall of his cell. His laboratory showed on the other side. Freedom was two feet away. He could smell the herbs he grew, their aroma filling his cell.

Before he could walk through the portal, a sharp pain formed in the upper portion of his back. Moving suddenly became difficult. The world spun and grew dark as he fell to the ground. He landed on his side, his arm on the other side of the portal he still had open. He struggled to stay connected to the Magic though he felt his strength fading. His legs stopped working. Why could he not move his legs? What had gone wrong? The portal closed, his arm still crossing into his laboratory. The pain he expected in his arm never came. Yet he watched the portal close and sever his arm just below the elbow. Why can't I feel that? Breathing became difficult, staggered. Something was wrong.

Chapter Eight

You utter bastard! I promised that you would die in that cell," the guard yelled as he started to stand against the far wall the spell knocked him into. Only the shield spell had saved him from the pure darkness the captive launched at him. A well-placed knife, thrown from across the room with the aid of some Magic, had stopped the madness. Now the Council would see the extent of this cult's power. Shame what happened to the warden, the guard thought to himself, as he took a quick look at the puddle that used to be a man.

The guard, using the wall for support, finally stood on his own. His back ached from his landing. The guard took a few steps before collapsing back to the floor, his vision growing dark, as he lay on the ground.

Chapter Nine

Roughly an hour later, the Councilors finally reached the dungeon, far beneath the College's main tower. The bloodbath that awaited them was something none of them could have predicted. Four of the seven total Councilors had come to hear what the captive had to say about this Assembly of Mages. It was an unsanctioned, unauthorized cult of ritualists that must be snuffed out at all costs. The dungeon, in its current state, was the only proof needed to make that decision. Still, the other Councilors would have to hear the arguments from those present and make their own decision. It wouldn't have to be a unanimous agreement, according to the bylaws of the College, but at least a majority had to agree. That could easily be done with those in this room alone.

Each Councilor examined something about the scene. One gazed, from a distance, at the scorched puddle on the floor, wondering what, or who, it had been before becoming liquified. Another looked over the captive, dead with a knife in his back. He also had no right arm just shy of his elbow. The information the captive had known was now lost, wiped away forever from the world. One Councilor examined the scorch marks left from what could only be wicked spells, the door to the cell melted by some unknown power.

"Could we have stopped this mage if he escaped?" one asked, looking closely at the bodies of the guards that had markings matching the door. "The spells he seems capable of casting are far beyond my understanding. How can we defend ourselves against something we know naught about?"

"There is strength in numbers, my brother Councilman," another replied, his answer sounding too bookish and lacking in reality.

"You were always the optimist, Carson. You are a fool if you think we could have stopped even just one of these dark mages," the first Councilor responded.

"I've seen enough. We must ban humanity from attending the College. Based on what I see here, they have strayed too far from our tenets and teachings, and therefore must now be punished. The human Councilors will understand once we present this evidence to them," one of the other Councilors said to the group, getting agreement from the others.

Ravens' Requiem

Chapter One

...Sometime in the Past...

A sweet, chilly wind blew through the town green and carried scents from all the fresh foods being cooked for the Celebration of Honey, the feast to mark the spring equinox. Bakers and cooks from around the village slaved away making many special foods for the occasion, and together their smells all conglomerated into a mass of sage, meats, vegetables, and a variety of other herbs. The entire town, including the guards, gathered in the green to celebrate the end of winter and the start of the planting season. Every year since the founding of Prikea this celebration happened on the first day of spring and the tradition seemed just as likely as ever that it would continue for years to come.

A small boy around the age of nine tugged at his mother's hand as they walked through the village green, his desires not set on food or drinks but on his friends who he could see were already busy playing. The young boy's name was Joshua and while his mother didn't try to restrain him, she did struggle to keep him at her side. Not far away from the spot on the green they selected, a group of children played with a ball and a wooden hoop which was only slightly bigger around than the ball itself. They were throwing the brown, leather ball back and forth between themselves and at various times they tried to get the ball to go through the hoop as another child held it.

The boy's father, Amos, placed a green and blue, plaid blanket on the ground and helped his wife, Shyla, place a few rocks, on the corners to hold the blanket down. Joshua started to run toward his friends again before Amos called to him; Joshua returned, sulking, to the blanket where he plopped down and pouted briefly and silently before turning to watch the other children as they played. He then turned to look at his father who was occupied by a basket and stood again. Amos quickly looked at Joshua.

"You can play when I leave to get our food, Joshua," he said.

"Yes, father," Joshua replied sadly.

Joshua sat on the blanket with his arms folded and his lower lip stuck out. He looked back to his friends. They were now chasing each other while the ball and hoop sat on the ground unused in the middle of their circle. He wanted to run around with them, but his father was being unfair making him stay on the blanket until they got food. Joshua didn't want food. He disliked veal stew and pork shoulder and he remembered that's all they had last year.

"Shyla, I'll return with food shortly. Keep an eye on the boy?" Amos said, standing then walking away from the blanket.

"Of course, my love," Shyla replied.

She turned to tell Joshua he could run and play, but the boy had already left the blanket, running toward his friends as fast as his legs would carry him. Shyla called to him and the boy stopped and turned around. She blew him a kiss, something which he disliked as his face went beet red before he continued running toward his friends. While he knew most of the children, like Douglas and Robert, there were others he hadn't met yet. He didn't care to learn their names right away, and based on the lack of questions, they didn't care to learn his either.

*   *   *

Joshua continued running around with his friends while the adults did boring things he hadn't cared about last year and still didn't care about now. Every so often while running around the ball and hoop he noticed something with candles in the center of the green and a man in white robes holding something up toward the sky. Joshua simply continued chasing his friends in circles until they turned around and chased him. This cycle continued until they all ended up sitting or lying on the ground, panting, and dripping sweat from their faces.

Douglas sat beside Joshua and laid down in the long grass as he stared at the sky, watching the various puffs of clouds waft by. Joshua fell backward and looked at the scattered clouds, trying to find his favorite. It was hard for him to pick; quite a few were good, but others were just plain clouds and those were boring.

"That one looks like a dragon!" Douglass shouted, pushing up onto his left elbow and pointing at a cloud far overhead.

"No, it looks like a basilisk, stupid," Joshua retorted.

"A basilisk *is* a dragon, Joshua."

"Who told you that?" Remy, the oldest boy in the group, asked.

"My uncle. He's one of the king's knights and knows everything about these things."

"Well, he doesn't know his arse from a hole in the ground," Remy countered, earning some giggles from the other children who seemed to be his friends.

"He does too! You're just jealous because someday I'll be a knight too!" Douglas proclaimed proudly, sitting up a hair straighter.

"Ha, in whose army?"

"The king's army, of course! I'll be the best knight in all the land," Douglas said.

"Yeah, the best at getting lost," Gregory cut in, getting a laugh from most of the others.

Douglas hung his head then looked to Joshua and spoke under his breath. "You believe me, don't you?"

"Of course. You'll be the best knight who ever—"

Before Joshua could finish his sentence there was a loud hiss, a pop, then the air grew hot and strong enough to push everything to the ground. Joshua tumbled around in a sloppy sort of somersault until he stopped on a sharp rock that lodged itself between his hip and his ribs. Another gust of strong wind shot from somewhere and the air felt hotter this time. His face tingled like when he played outside too long. He tried to look around, but the gusts were too strong to resist and he kept getting knocked back into the ground before he could sit up.

Screams filled the air around them. Many of the adults, also pinned to the ground, yelled, and tried to look around at what was going on. Others seemed able to stand and were running with the gusts of wind. Douglas shrieked nearby and Joshua rolled over to see what was going on. The oak tree they had been playing near had fallen and a branch had landed on his friend's legs, pinning him to the ground. His cries drowned out some of the adults nearby. Joshua felt a pit forming in his stomach before a bright flash of white light came from near the food tables and spread over the group of people, some on the ground, some still standing. Joshua looked away because his eyes hurt from the intensity of the light.

In an instant, the white light was gone, and Joshua felt hotter than he ever felt before. His ears rang with a high-pitched screeching. His vision swirled and everything around him spun like someone took the world and shook it. Everything spun, his vision blurred, and he could hardly see anything. He looked around, hoping for something he could make out as a familiar shape, but nothing came into focus. The gusts of wind had stopped by now, and he finally felt like he could sit up. When he tried, his vision shifted and everything around him seemed to jump. His stomach disliked this turn of events and picked that moment to empty itself of his breakfast. He felt the warm splashes on his hands and legs before he fell back onto the ground.

Chapter Two

Joshua woke up sweating and panting. His breath caught in his chest and he coughed before sitting up in his bed. He looked around his room, the shadows from the spartan furniture casting strange shapes throughout the room. His chair, sitting in the corner by his wardrobe, looked occupied and Joshua cast two spells, one which illuminated the room and the other, which he held back in his hand, was a blast of air ready to stun any unwelcome visitors sitting in his room. The Priests forbade dangerous spells outside of exercise time and he didn't want to get in trouble, so he hadn't started a fire spell this time. Thankfully, the blast of air would also clap like thunder, alarming anyone within the nearby rooms and send them running. This wouldn't be neither the first time for that sound to echo through the monastery, nor the last.

The ball of light which appeared in the center of the room above Joshua's bed showed nothing in the chair but a former shadow caught on the nearby wardrobe. Joshua carefully released his spell. He had not been so careful in the past and Francis gave him a stern talking to about the dangers of reckless Magic usage. He had since avoided another lecture but given that in the morning Joshua would become a member of the Order of Ravens, he really didn't want to take any chances with spells.

With his investigation and spellcasting done, Joshua returned to the matter at hand. He wiped a palmful of sweat from his brow and wiped his hand on his pajama trousers before standing and moving to the washbasin. He filled the simple clay bowl with water from a nearby pitcher, then used a simple spell to heat the water ever so slightly; thin tendrils of steam rose from the surface of the water. Joshua grabbed a small towel then dipped a corner of it into the basin then wiped the cold sweat from his bald head, arms, and bare chest. He continued dipping the towel into the water until he felt clean and now cold as the water air-dried on his skin. Joshua splashed his face with water, turned to his wardrobe, grabbed his outercoat, threw it on, and stepped out into the dim hallway outside his room.

He wandered the grounds of the monastery, slowly walking up one hallway and down another until he found himself in the courtyard with an olive tree in the center. The single bench under the tree was already occupied, so Joshua stayed toward the edge of the courtyard, not wanting to disrupt the other priest's meditation. Many of his soon-to-be brothers came to the courtyard for meditation before their days started with the rise of the sun. Despite his efforts to remain silent, however, he was soon greeted by a kind voice he could recognize even in the darkest of rooms: Francis.

"You should be resting, my son," Francis said from the bench without turning around.

"I couldn't sleep," Joshua replied truthfully.

"Why tell me something obvious? I can see by your presence here and now that you had trouble sleeping."

"I had a nightmare. I haven't experienced this dream in many years, and I don't know why it's coming back," Joshua replied.

"Come and sit with me for a moment," Francis invited.

"I don't want to disturb your time meditating," Joshua declined.

"Nonsense. That's what I'm here for. Many of the others come to me with things they don't understand or have yet to comprehend. Tell me of this nightmare you had."

"It was about that day," Joshua started, feeling a lump in his throat already.

"The Celebration of Honey?"

"Yes. Again, I haven't had these dreams since I was a young man and at the time I figured they were caused by the trauma. Now, though, I'm unsure," Joshua said, taking a seat on the stone bench next to Francis.

"Many would still consider you a young man, Joshua. Could it be that you're nervous about what happens in the morning? This is quite a commitment you're about to make to us and the Allfather," Francis said, scratching at the scruff on his chin.

"I don't think so. This felt more real than other nervous dreams. I could smell the heat in the air, my eyes blurred, and the ground shifted beneath my feet. It was too real to just be my nerves talking. Those dreams always feel uncertain and fake, like there is something wrong with the reality in them," Joshua explained.

"Such vivid dreams can tell us more about ourselves than perhaps we would like. What could this mean? What is similar between that day and this?" Francis asked.

"There *is* a big change coming," Joshua answered quickly.

"That would mean this is nerves and nothing more. I recommend you take some time and meditate, then get some more rest while you still can. Dawn is still a few hours away," Francis reminded. "You should focus on the wonder and might of the Allfather instead of things that plague this mortal body in which we reside."

"I will do that," Joshua said. "Can you recommend anything specific that will help? The dreams still feel so vivid I don't know if I can focus on anything else."

"Clear your mind as we have taught you, Joshua. You have all the tools you have at your disposal," Francis suggested.

"I understand. Thank you," Joshua said, standing from the stone bench and walking toward the door that led out from the interior courtyard. His sandal-clad feet crunched softly on the gravel as he walked back toward the maze of hallways in the monastery.

"Brother Joshua," Francis called from the bench, "get some rest. Tomorrow is a big day for you."

"Of course. Thank you for the reminder, Francis."

Joshua left the courtyard and returned down the path of hallways toward his room where he changed the blankets on his bed, leaving the sweat-soaked ones on his chair where he would find them in the morning. With new covers on his bed, Joshua knelt on the floor and cleared his mind as he had learned some years ago during the early stages of his journey toward priesthood. He emptied all emotions, thoughts, desires, and fears from his mind until his presence was left floating in a void where a singular light guided him toward his goal: peace. The light, he knew, was the Allfather's presence and he reached for it, longed for it, desired it. Everything within him yearned for that light…until a shadow moved in the way.

It felt cold, ugly, sad. Something was wrong with the shadow. It blocked his way but then it moved to the side. Even in the emptiness of the abyss, he could sense its presence, could see it as it rippled like the light, could feel the reflections of the light bouncing off its shimmering surface. He stopped, floating once again in his mind, and reached for the shadow, stretched for it, *hoped* for it. He turned away from the light and moved toward the shadow until its bone-chilling touch began to ease over him. He jolted and backed away, returning toward the light and its glorious warmth once again. He stopped, merely a presence in his mind, and weighed his options. In the mesmerizing surface of the shadow, he could see images of the day he lost his parents. Joshua could feel the pain, the loss, the terror as he rushed to Douglas's side and his friend refused to move under his touch. He could smell the sulfur from the Magic-based fire burning nearby. He felt the dizziness of that day after the shockwave of the immolation spell shook his village to its core. Despite all those sensations, he longed for the darkness, desired to see what truths it concealed behind its always-moving surface. The Allfather's light seemed so far away. So distant now that it felt cold. The shadow, by contrast, now felt warm and welcoming. Joshua reached for it once again.

"Do not stray from the Allfather's light," a voice boomed in his mind.

"What? Who's there?" Joshua felt his voice quiver through the abyss he had created.

"Do not stray from the Allfather's light. Your time has not yet come," the voice said again, the deep, commanding presence of it filling every bit of space within Joshua's mind.

Joshua opened his eyes and gasped as his emotions and everything else flooded back into his mind in an instant. His heart pounded and his temples throbbed. He had learned as part of this exercise that leaving the abyss too quickly caused mild sickness and migraines. The first time he had left his mind in a rush he spent about an hour throwing up and the next two days in bed recovering from the worst headache he had experienced up to that point in his life. Simon and Gerald, two of the other priests, received a stern talk from Francis for not warning him about the void before teaching him how to get there. As punishment, they tended to Joshua during his days of resting.

This time, however, Joshua recovered relatively quickly, only staggering on his knees for a brief moment before he was fine. His stomach lurched but nothing came back up and his heartbeat returned to its normal speed within a minute which also stopped the pounding at his temples. He leaned forward, planting his hands on the ground, and pushed himself up to stand at his full height. Joshua stretched and rolled his head to the left then quickly to the right, feeling a couple of small pops in his neck followed by one big pop which felt great.

Joshua knelt again, once more clearing his mind of everything and entering the void where the only thing that remained was the Allfather's light. Just as before, something seemed to be blocking the brilliance of it. The obstruction moved and Joshua looked at it once again, seeing it was the darkness he started reaching toward. He kept watching it and again saw the images of his parents and friends, those he had loved before that fateful Celebration of Honey that left him utterly alone in this life. Priests. He belonged to the priesthood now. They took him in after the attack and gave him a second family. Each of them had been like brothers to him for so much of his life. Joshua felt the void in his mind shiver and shake as the darkness started to roil and bubble, growing in size before he once again snapped out of his meditation. Everything within him ached now, as he fell toward the floor, only just catching himself with his elbow before his head hit the plain, scratchy rug in the center of his room. He panted once again and used his hand to wipe more sweat from his brow. Beads of sweat dripped down his hand as he wiped it on the leg of his trousers, leaving several dark streaks.

Joshua went to his washbasin again and used another spell to heat the water just enough for a few tendrils of steam to rise from the surface of the water. He grabbed the same small towel, but this time dipped the whole thing in the water, leaving his hands under the surface as the heat seeped in and soothed him. He removed the towel, wrang out much of the excess, and placed the cloth on his face, breathing in the steam and heat for just a moment. He wiped down his face as well as the top and back of his head before dunking the cloth back into the water which had cooled off enough to be unpleasant. Again, he wrang the excess water from the cloth and wiped down his chest and arms then returned the cloth to the bowl one last time to rinse it.

Freshly cleaned, Joshua returned to his bed, leaving the down-filled blanket cast aside. He cut the spell that still illuminated the room and blinked as nearly total darkness enveloped him. Trying to fall asleep again, he stared at a spot on the ceiling above his bed and thought of what was to come with his life in the priesthood. It was a well-kept secret throughout the continent that the priests were Mages. After the Evacuation of Drendil many years before, the other continents still harbored a distrust for Mages. The attack on Prikea during the Celebration of Honey had not helped. Unfortunately, not much was known or taught about Drendil anymore. Joshua assumed Madness still ruled the land there. He shuddered at the thought of so much Dark Magic that it caused actual Madness.

Joshua's eyes grew heavy as he stared at the ceiling and speculated about the other continents. He had learned some about Ofari, Istraes, and Udin but not nearly as much as he learned about Prikea. It made sense to him, though. He lived in Prikea, so of course, he learned more about this land than the others. He closed his eyes and tried to picture the world from high above but drifted off to sleep before he could get very far above the ground.

Chapter Three

...Sometime in the Past...

Screaming. Adults calling the names of children, children crying for their parents. Joshua knelt on the ground beside Douglas who was still pinned under a section of the broken oak tree. The other boy had grown quiet and still, his face starting to pale. Joshua didn't know what to do. He touched his friend on the shoulder, but nothing happened. Douglas was simply looking at the sky, his eyes not blinking anymore. Blood that stained the corners of his mouth and his top lip under his nose getting crusty.

Joshua felt one single tear drop from his eye and land on his hand. His parents hadn't talked to him about death yet, thinking it best that he didn't find out about that until later in life. Part of him understood it in this moment, kneeling beside his friend who looked so peaceful now. Douglas had been screaming a lot and Joshua tried to help him but wasn't strong enough to pick up the piece or the tree. Joshua's ears were still ringing, and things still sounded garbled like when he had gone swimming before and tried to talk underwater. This felt different though.

Joshua finally looked away from his friend, his head turning around, looking for where his parents had been the last time he saw them. He quickly spotted the blue and green plaid blanket they brought with them for the equinox picnic and ran toward it. None of the rocks they put on the corners of the blanket were there. The wicker basket with their dishes and silverware was nowhere to be seen. His mother wasn't there. He continued looking around, feeling panic boiling up inside him. Other adults walked around here and there throughout the village green, but he didn't see his parents. Screaming. He could hear the screaming clearly, even with the garbled sounds in his ears.

He sat on the blanket and felt more tears flood from his eyes, streaming down his face. The tears felt cold against his hot face. He didn't know how much time passed while he knelt on the blanket sobbing, but soon enough it grew dark and the sun dropped to the horizon. Everything started growing chilly without the heat of the sun overhead bearing down on the town green. Joshua didn't care about that. He only felt despair and pain. Physical pain. His face and hands stung from the hot blasts of air that knocked him down before the blinding flash of light. He clasped his hands together and held them in his lap, leaning forward. A little pressure on the backs of his hands felt nice, and he used the insides of his legs to apply more until he found the point where it started feeling worse before easing back.

"My dear child," a soothing voice said from behind him. "Where are your parents?"

Joshua looked up and turned to the voice and found a man wearing tan robes with a black raven embroidered on the chest. His sleeves bore several stripes on them of the same color. His eyes and smile were both friendly and welcoming and he reached out his hand toward Joshua, who would have normally shied away from a stranger, but he felt so cold and empty inside that he didn't care anymore. He reached out his hand and put it in the man's smooth hand. The stranger helped him stand then looked him over.

"Were you in the attack earlier? What did you see?" he asked Joshua.

"There was a light that hurt," Joshua answered.

"That's what we thought happened. I can explain what happened here when you are older, but I think first we should find your parents. Do you know where they are?"

Joshua pointed first at the picnic blanket he stood on, then toward broken tree nearby. "Mother was here when I went to play with my friends over there."

"And your father? Where was he?"

"Getting food for us."

"Have you seen them around here?" he asked.

"No. I've been here since before it got dark, but they haven't come back," Joshua said.

"My dear child, I'm so sorry," the man said to Joshua.

The man knelt and embraced Joshua. As the man's hands touched his shoulder, Joshua felt a coolness rush across his shoulders and the stinging in his face and hands went away before the man let him go and looked him in the eyes. His face seemed very concerned.

"What is your name, child?"

"Joshua."

"I'm sorry, Joshua, but I don't believe your parents are here anymore. We can look for them if you would like, but I don't think we will find them."

"Where are they?" Joshua asked.

"I believe the Allfather is guiding them home now, child."

"Like my friend, Douglas?"

"Where is Douglas?"

"He's over there, under the tree."

"Stay right here," the man said before jogging over to the broken tree.

He stopped and put his hand over his mouth in what looked like shock then made a motion and knelt beside Douglas. He did something that Joshua couldn't see because of the tree branch in the way, then returned. His face looked more upset than it had before.

"Yes, I believe your parents, and Douglas, are with the Allfather now," the man said.

"What do I do now?"

"You can come with me. I'm a priest here in Prikea. My brothers and I will take care of you and teach you what you need to know. I can tell you are a very special boy already."

"What do you mean?"

"You have a gift that not so many have these days, Joshua."

"What gift is that?" Joshua asked.

"We can discuss that more when the time comes. Would you like to meet my brothers?"

"Are they also priests?"

"They are, and they will help me with taking care of you."

"Ok. Where are they?"

Chapter Four

...The Present Day...

Joshua woke up as the sky outside his window started turning grey with the approach of sunrise. He blinked and stared at the ceiling before tossing aside his covers, once again soaked in sweat. He placed his feet on the floor beside his bed and felt the chilly tinge of the floor through the thin, scratchy rug. He walked to his wardrobe, opened the doors, and removed the new robes that identified him as a full member of the Order of Ravens. They were simple tan robes with a black raven embroidered on the chest and stripes of the same color on the cuffs of the sleeves. These robes were the same as Francis wore the day of the attack.

He hung the robes on the open door of his wardrobe and walked over to the washbasin, still full of water, and used a spell to heat the water for the third time. He used the same small towel from earlier and washed away the drying sweat from his face, scalp, chest, and arms before removing his trousers and slipping on his new robes.

The fabric of his new priest robes felt stiff as he slipped into them. These robes were what he would wear for the duration of his time in the Order. He looked in the mirror on the inside of the wardrobe door and inspected his reflection as he finished getting ready for his induction ceremony. This would be a small gathering for just the Order members and himself. The way Francis explained it, this would work like any of the other services they held for the people of Prikea, but with the focus being on servitude and dedication to the people and the Allfather rather than praise for the creator of life.

He finished preparing his robes and as he did, a glint of a memory came back to him from the night before. While meditating he had reached out and attempted to touch the darkness that obscured the Allfather's light. He had never seen anything like that before and wondered if something like that would happen again. Maybe that was a one-time thing. *It did happen twice last night, though*, he reminded himself. Joshua felt beads of sweat forming on his forehead and wiped them away with his towel before they dripped onto his clean robes.

Joshua finished preparing for the induction ceremony and left his room for a refreshing walk in the chilly morning air. A gentle breeze rolled through the monastery and he breathed in the air which carried a hint of lilacs from the nearby prairie. He wandered toward the courtyard and sat on the same stone bench beneath the tree from his earlier talk with Francis. Here he could see over the monastery wall into the nearby fields, and he watched as the sun slowly rose from his left and illuminated the grasses and wildflowers. Deer, looking for their morning meals, sprang through the tall grass, bouncing as happily as they could. Joshua sighed, wondering what his life would have been like had the attack hadn't happened at the Celebration of Honey all those years ago. He likely wouldn't have started practicing Magic nor would he have joined the Order of Ravens. His life started pretty rockily because of that day, but he knew now things were for the best.

*   *   *

The induction ceremony, a service held only for members of the Order of Ravens, past or present, was indeed simple, as Francis had described it. Gerald, the next newest member of the Order, read a passage from the scripture that talked about service to others, and Francis, the head of the Order, lit a series of candles on the altar as the passage was read. Only eight people gathered in the monastery, one a previous member of the Order and the other seven were the current members. Francis, Simon, Peter, Gerald, Oliver, William, and Joshua stood before the altar with Joshua at the center of the group and Francis on his right. Francis raised his hands, palms up, toward the ceiling, and started speaking.

"Allfather, we gather here before you to bring a member into our fold, following your divine direction. Guide him as you have guided us. Allfather above, guide us toward your will," Francis started and paused.

"Bring us peace," Simon said from Joshua's left.

"Lead us to your people," Gerald said, as he also raised his hands.

"Carry us when we are weak," Oliver said, his hands raised.

"Feed us when we have nothing," William said.

"Clothe us when we are bare," Peter said.

"And allow us to protect those around us from the ways of evil," Joshua said, finishing the Order's creed.

"Welcome to the Order of Ravens, Brother Joshua," Francis said, embracing him.

The Manticore

Chapter One

Time passed as it always had. Some days felt shorter than some, yet others seemed to stretch for an eternity. Regardless of that sensation, each day began and ended the same way. With the sun rising over the eastern horizon in brilliant displays of color and falling beyond the western skyline.

Nearly three months had come and gone since the Siege of Shemont, as the battle between the army of Drendil and the army of monsters assembled by Vor'Kath had come to be named. In that time the city's gate, found west of the castle, had been replaced. The breach in the southern portion of the city's wall was well underway, repairs coming further along each day.

The Siege had changed many things within the city, though some of those changes were subtle, invisible changes. The king was under much scrutiny by his people, many of whom were unhappy with his departure right before the attack started. Some citizens saw the necessity for him to leave, yet others argued that a king was supposed to be the first and last on the battlefield. Shemont had nearly fallen into turmoil after the attack, more so than it had during.

Sir Michael the Valiant, Knight-Captain of the Royal Order of Drendil jogged into the castle as he had many days since the Siege. Today, he was scheduled to meet with the king right before midday to discuss a matter about which he had little information. He hated getting caught off guard with things. All he knew is the king wished to discuss an assignment with him, something he was excited to tackle. He had been growing tired sitting in his estate. This would be his first real assignment from the King since gaining his knighthood.

As a Knight-Captain he had been assigned a squire, a wonderful man by the name of George, who saw to every wish and desire that Michael had or could find. Michael still wasn't used to being waited on, and it bothered him. Not too long ago, he had been a carpenter's apprentice. Now, he was a man of status, a Knight-Captain. Soldiers saluted him, as they had since he was appointed the rank of lieutenant in the army, but now those salutes seemed to carry *more* respect than they had before. Perhaps the soldiers knew he was not a born-knight and had instead worked his way to that status. One thing he knew was different between him and other knights was his lack of a signet ring, something he hoped to change someday.

Once inside the castle, Michael went up a spiraling staircase, and walked up two levels before he exited, turned right down a long corridor then entered another staircase. After climbing another level, he turned left and counted four doors before he arrived at the Master General's office. The oak door was simple except for five six-pointed stars carved into the top center of the wooden surface. While he had once learned what each of the stars represented, he had since forgotten. As he walked in front of the door, it opened and the king walked out, closing the door behind him.

"Ah, Sir Michael, I was hoping you would be here soon. As you know, I have an assignment for you. I think you'll enjoy this," the king said, making a motion for Michael to follow him.

"Is this assignment for just me, or can I have Joshua come with me?" Michael asked.

"This is just for you. I believe Joshua is busy with some research or something along those lines. He still wants to find out all he can about the mysterious hand you both said took Týr and Vor'Kath away at the end of the battle," the king stated as he opened the door to his office.

Michael waited for the king to take a seat before taking one himself. Then, seeing the older man grab his pipe, Michael retrieved his own and filled it carefully from a new bag of tobacco leaves he had gotten from George. The smell of citrus struck his nose upon opening the pouch and the smell only grew stronger as he pulled out a pinch of the leaves and packed them tightly into the bottom of the bowl. Then, using his thumb and finger, made a ball of the semi-moist leaves and placed the ball into the bowl of his pipe. This he topped with some loose leaves before striking a match and lighting the leaves on fire. From the corner of his eye, he could see the king watching him, his pipe held idly between his teeth.

"That's an interesting technique. Any reason you pack your pipe that way?" he finally asked when Michael stopped and looked up.

"I have found it burns better this way. And I can avoid relighting the tobacco as the ball holds all the heat that I need," Michael answered. "Highness…"

"You can leave the formalities at the door for these kinds of meetings, Michael. Please, call me Orson," he requested.

"Sire, I cannot call you anything informal. It feels wrong," Michael protested. Even hearing the king's name without any titles sounded wrong.

"I understand that. I figured I would extend the offer," Orson stated. "Now, we should discuss this assignment I have for you. As I'm sure you're aware, Vor'Kath had amassed an army of monsters, some of which we have never dealt with before. I remember you mentioning that you and Týr fought a manticore in the courtyard, is that correct?"

"Yes, Highness," Michael replied.

"Good! So, you have experience dealing with the beasts. It may not be much experience, but it's more than many of my knights.

There is a village about a day and a half ride northwest of here named Haran. They have complained, through their village elder, about a manticore that keeps attacking them every few days. They have lost much of their livestock, which is essential to the kingdom, both our side and the Elves. They are one of the largest sources of beef and milk that we have, and lately, we have had a shortage, all thanks to this monster. I need you to go deal with it," Orson requested.

"Highness, I'm sure there are other knights who are far better suited for this task than I am," Michael said.

"Well, there is one knight that I would have given this assignment to, but he fights too aggressively for something like this. And there is the matter of not knowing where he is at the moment," Orson alluded.

"And who would that be?"

"Týr, Michael. We have no idea where he is, or if he is even still alive."

"I understand… I accept this assignment, Highness," Michael replied, feeling embarrassed to have forgotten about his comrade disappearing into a mysterious hole in the sky with Vor'Kath only a few months prior.

"Good. The village should be very welcoming, especially if you can deal with this problem of theirs. Now, if you are done smoking your pipe, you should get going. See me when you are finished," Orson requested.

Chapter Two

Michael rode his gelding, Watson, hard the next day, hoping to arrive in Haran before sunset. He could see the village less than a league away. He spurred his gelding to a gallop and tucked himself as far as he could, riding faster across the plains. His horse snorted under the command and moved faster, panting as it galloped toward the village as fast as it could.

With only a kilometer left, Michael slowed his horse down to a trot. Watson whinnied when he was able to slow down and again when Michael climbed out of the saddle and walked the horse by the reins. He rewarded the horse with an apple, he had packed in a saddlebag. Watson munched contentedly on the fruit and swished his tail back and forth.

Walking into the village, Michael surveyed the place. To the west and south were sparse trees that eventually became a small forest. If he was correctly recalling the map he had studied, this was the same forest Týr and his late sister Svenka had lived in as thieves before leaving that life behind them and going to Erith. Remembering Týr brought pain to Michael, still not sure if his comrade was alive, or where he even had gone after that great dark hand had grabbed Vor'Kath out of the courtyard a few months before.

To the north of the village rose a few mountains, though none of them were particularly great. Unlike other mountains that Michael had seen, or even grown up around, these mountains sported no snow on their peaks, something that made them seem so…foreign. His home city of Feldring had been built into the side of great mountains that were always snow-capped, no matter the time of year. Having grown up in that environment, he figured that all mountains would be snowy.

As he approached the village, a flock of people gathered and ran to meet him. Some of them ran, at least. Many of those were children, excited to see someone new coming to their troubled hamlet. The children crowded around him but kept their distance, somehow excited to see him and unsure at the same time. The crowd around him parted as a wizened man approached, walking with a tall stave which was knotty and bent in places, much as the man himself was. This had to be the village elder he was supposed to meet and discuss their issues with the manticore.

"Greeting, Knight! Welcome to Haran. My name is Yoska and I am the Elder here. We have pled for so long for the king to send someone to help us. We are plagued by evil, good knight. Please help us rid this evil from our land," the man begged.

"Yoska, I have indeed been sent to help. Is there a stable for my horse? We should also discuss this matter in private if that is fine with you," Michael suggested.

"Why should it be private? We all know a monster has attached itself to our lands. We lose cattle every few days. It started as only one heifer at a time, but lately, it has been more than that," one of the villagers called from the back of the crowd. The man had a plain face and a haircut that, while simple, somehow also seemed ridiculous. It appeared that he had had a bowl set on top of his head and then had cut whatever had stuck out from under the bowl. Only the bowl in question would have been a few sizes too small for the man. His hair barely reached his slightly too-big ears.

"This monster, we believe, is a manticore. The king has made this determination based on—" Michael started but got cut off.

"We don't care what it's called, or why you call it that. We only want the thing dead!" another villager shouted.

"Now, now. Let's not be rude. This beast has found its way here, but it is not the fault of…" Yoska looked at Michael for his name.

"Sir Michael the Valiant."

"Pah! We'll see about that!" a woman called from his left.

"Alamina, watch your tongue. I assume Sir Michael has earned his title the same as every other knight in Drendil. He is here to help us with our problem, not make it worse. Let's show him some hospitality while he deals with this monster," Yoska scolded.

"Again, is there a stable for my horse? I will also need to see the innkeeper about a room if there is one available," Michael stated calmly. He had a hard time believing that *this* was the reception he was getting from the village.

"We have an inn by the name of the Chubby Owl. There are but two rooms there, and either of them are available for you, Sir Michael. Please follow me and we will speak with Milosh about your needs," Yoska stated, waving for Michael to follow him. One of the villagers, who Michael guessed was a stable hand, grabbed Watson's reins and led him off to the north, toward the mountains.

Michael followed Yoska to the Chubby Owl, a small, thatched-roof building with a small garden in the front and a split-rail fence around. Michael looked around the village and saw many of the buildings had been built in the same style. He didn't see one building with a proper roof, they were all thatched. The door to the inn stood open, and a large man stood in the doorway. He was easily two meters tall with a potbelly and what appeared to be very little of a neck. This made Michael wonder if perhaps Milosh was the inspiration for the inn's name.

"Greetings, friend!" the man called from the doorway.

"Greetings," Michael replied. "I need a room for a few days."

"It's yours if you can rid us of this beast. I can give you up to a week for that feat," Milosh promised. "Anything beyond that'll be a silver a day."

"That sounds good," Michael said, nearly choking when he heard the price. Inns in Shemont were expensive and often cost a gold mark a day. He had assumed all inns in the area would charge similar rates, and he was pleased to find less costly accommodations.

Yoska bowed then walked away, using his knotty stave for support as he shuffled down the packed-dirt road. Michael walked into the Chubby Owl and Milosh pointed to the two doors at the back of the dining area. After a quick check, both rooms were identical, so Michael had no way of really deciding which room he wanted. Not wanting to cause an issue, he picked the right room and set down his bow, quiver, and sword before returning to the dining area to speak with Milosh. He didn't intend to stay up much longer. He needed to get some sleep and prepare for the next day. He would get up early and start hunting this manticore.

In the dining area, Milosh offered him some beef and vegetable stew, something which smelled divine. Michael ate two bowls and a few pieces of thick-crusted bread which went well with the stew. His evening meal finished, Michael stretched and returned to his room, stretching out on the bed before drifting to sleep without taking off his armor.

Chapter Three

Michael started from his sleep hearing some sort of commotion outside. He initially figured it was nothing, but after trying to go back to sleep he heard bestial roars that brought back memories of the Siege when the manticore had flown into the courtyard. It sounded like a large cat was right outside his room, but he knew that was impossible. Likely the beast was flying overhead though he doubted that would also be an issue. Michael jumped out of bed and grabbed his weaponry, rushing out of the Chubby Owl to get a better idea of the situation.

There it was. The manticore. It flew over the village in circles. Its roars were just as Michael remembered: fierce and haunting. It was as if someone had put a man's voice inside a lion's body, gave it wings and a scorpion's tail, and set loose the conglomeration of animal parts. This particular manticore was larger than the last one he had faced. During the Siege, he and Týr had fought one that was maybe a meter tall at the shoulders. This one had to be nearly thrice that size! It's wings, though he couldn't judge them well as they were flapping and it was dark, had to be eight or ten meters across from tip to tip. Given just the sheer size of this creature, this assignment would be unpleasant, but at least it was here now and could be dealt with quickly.

Michael strung his bow and grabbed an arrow from his quiver, which he had thrown on the back of his belt, so it rested in the small of his back. He nocked the arrow on the string and waited for the manticore to stop circling. When it finally noticed him, the monster flew overhead and circled back before landing in the middle of the dirt road. When it flew overhead the wind from its wings blew up dust and bits of small stones from the surface of the road. The monster charged toward Michael, giving him hardly any time to draw his bow. He managed to get the arrow brought back before releasing it, but with his haste, he failed to draw the bow back enough and the arrow only flew a couple of meters before falling short of the manticore.

The beast was quick, despite its size, and Michael had to dash to his right to get out of its path. While it was quick, it was not agile, and the tight layout of the village was too much for the manticore to be able to turn around and chase after Michael, who was now drawing his bow again, ensuring he drew the arrow back far enough this time. He touched the first knuckle of his thumb against the edge of his chin and released the arrow. The bow responded with a *twang* as the arrow sailed through the air toward the manticore, who had turned around and was again heading in Michael's direction. The arrow contacted and bounced off the monster's man-like face, which made the creature roar in anger. This revealed its many rows of sharp teeth, something Michael had not expected to see. Angered by the attack, the monster pounced, leaping toward Michael, who dodged out of the way of its massive paws.

Standing after recovering from his dodge, he drew his sword and spun toward the massive predator, bringing the sword down toward its front left paw. The creature howled as the sword dug into its thick hide. Blood gushed from the wound, though Michael thought it was too minor to cause harm.

Before Michael could recover from his attack, the monster used the outside of its now-wounded paw and swiped Michael away, launching him into the side of a nearby house. The force of slamming into the house knocked all the wind from his lungs, and he felt something in his back cracking, though he wasn't sure what that had been. Or if he had even felt anything at all.

As Michael sat on the ground and leaned against the house, slowly recovering his breath, he watched the manticore take a step toward him, the massive lion's paw flattening as it pressed into the dirt. The paw itself had to be damn near a meter wide, Michael thought. This was a huge creature, there was no doubt about that. The manticore's tail raised, rearing back as if to strike Michael.

Chapter Four

A horn sounded from the east. A rich timber pealed through the village of Haran as Michael watched the manticore, startled by the sound, back away. Finally recovered, Michael stood and grabbed his sword from where it had landed nearby. The beast was distracted, and this seemed to be the most opportune time to strike. As he raised his sword, a sharp pain struck just below his right shoulder blade, sending a shockwave through his arm and down his back. He dropped his sword and heard the steel ping against a stone.

The horn sounded again and the manticore jumped into the air and flapped its mighty wings. The ensuing gust forced Michael back into the wall of the house. As it flew away, Michael watched the monster turn and head for the nearest of the mountains, where it likely had been living since the Siege. After the sun came up, he would make his way there and hunt down the beast and earn the reward the king has mentioned before he left the castle.

Free from danger, Michael took his time recovering. While he tried to stand, suddenly weary from that short fight, the female villager who lived in the house he had been knocked into came out and helped him stand up. This surprised Michael as she was older than other villagers he had seen, except Yoska, and hunched over. Her round, olive face showed the signs of countless years of working fields, and when she smiled at him, he saw she was missing all but a few of her front teeth. The elderly woman grabbed his sword for him, once he was on his feet, and offered to return it to his scabbard. Michael thanked her but refused, thinking that would be too much help. He was fine, he thought.

His things gathered, Michael turned his attention to the direction of the horn, and the approaching rider. By the look of the armor, it was another knight! And one from Shemont by the crimson tabard with a golden griffon emblazoned on the front. From this distance, Michael could see the rider wore the steel armor that many other knights seemed to prefer. Personally, Michael preferred lighter armor as it seemed to give him more range of motion and didn't weigh him down during a fight. That preference might have come from his time in the army patrolling the streets of Shemont.

The rider approached and Michael could see the newly arrived knight was a woman! He hadn't thought many women were knighted, but that was no reason to not welcome her. As she drew close, she reined in her horse, a stallion, of all things, climbed out of her saddle, and removed her helmet, a simple steel helmet with a pair of wings attached to the sides. Michael thought that was a useless addition for a helmet, especially if the wings ever got caught on anything. Michael started to take a step toward the other knight, but she held up her hand, motioning for him to stay where he was.

"You're welcome," she said, her voice sporting a touch of Elven lilt.

"What?" Michael asked.

"I just saved your life. That monster was about to spear you with its tail. I have seen them before, and they move as fast as a lightning strike. You would have died, citizen," she explained.

Confused, Michael looked down and examined what he was wearing, not sure why she was talking to him like he was a lowly village patrolman. He saw the same golden griffon that she wore and grew even more confused. He was covered in dirt, but the griffon was still visible.

"I'm not a citizen. I'm Sir Michael the Valiant," he corrected.

"*You're* a knight? Unbelievable. It seems that Orson is giving the title to anyone he wishes these days, regardless of their combat experience. What lineage are you from?" she inquired. Her voice no longer carried the lilt it once had.

"I'm not from any of the lineages. I'm from Prikea. I fought at the Siege of Shemont and was knighted for my efforts there. Surely, you've heard of that!" Michael protested. He didn't even know her name, but this other knight was already getting on his nerves talking to him like a commoner.

"I have heard of that. I was away on business or I would have been there to protect the city," she claimed. "Were you on the frontlines during the battle or something? How did you come to be knighted?"

"I was fighting the Vor that led the Siege…" Michael started but was cut off.

"Bullshit! You couldn't even handle yourself against that manticore. There's no way you fought a Vor and lived…"

"Listen here…" Michael started, taking a step toward the other knight. It was at this time she dropped her helmet and brought her armored fist into Michael's stomach, knocking the wind from his lungs for the second time that evening.

Michael didn't give himself the time he needed to recover and instead threw himself into the other knight, dragging her to the ground with him. Once on the ground, he thought he would have an advantage in this sudden fight but instead caught a gauntlet-covered fist with his mouth. His bottom lip felt warm and wet, telling him she had split it open.

Before Michael could react, he felt himself getting lifted from under his arms and hauled backward. He had no idea who was holding him, but the other knight was also being held by a couple of the villagers who had likely come out of their homes after the manticore flew off. A man appeared between the two knights with his hands reached out toward both of them.

"Now, what appears to be the problem here?" the man asked. Michael noticed a star-shaped badge was pinned to the simple, black vest that he wore over a threadbare shirt.

"He was going to attack me, I simply defended myself," the other knight claimed.

"I took a step forward and she punched me! And she scared off the manticore I'm here to kill," Michael corrected.

"You're on assignment?!" the other spat.

"Stop, both of you. Now, I didn't see how this started, but this is how it ends. Either you will be civil toward each other, or we will ask you to leave. Sir Michael was here first, my lady. And it sounds like the king has sent him here to help us with our problem. This is his hunt. Can you accept these terms?" the man asked.

"No. This man attacked me and is falsely claiming knighthood. He can't even fight a simple manticore without almost dying. How is he a knight?" the other spat.

"Well, my lady, we will have to ask you to leave Haran for right now. Please grab your things and go," the man with the star on his vest said.

"By what authority do you ask me to leave?" the knight asked.

"I am the village marshal. Other than the elder's own words, what I say is the law. Please, leave our village in peace," the marshal requested again, this time more firmly than before.

"Fine. Have your dogs release me," the knight asked, still being held by the villagers who had grabbed her. The villages released her and Michael at the same time. Michael then wiped his mouth with the back of his hand, finding blood was indeed coming from his lip.

"Come with me, Sir Michael. I will get your wound patched up before you retire again for the evening," Yoska said from behind him.

Michael was surprised to find the wizened old man standing behind him. He would have figured the elder would have spoken up while the marshal was handling the scuffle he and the other knight had gotten into. Instead, he seemed to allow people to perform their duties as they were supposed to, something Michael could respect from a leader.

Yoska walked toward a small thatched-roof building, built the same as all the others in Haran, but smaller than the rest. Michael followed and once inside the hut, Yoska motioned to a stool for Michael to sit on. He obeyed and the elder set down his stave then shuffled over to his visitor. Without warning, his hand glowed a soft white, something Michael had become familiar with after the few years he had known Joshua. Yoska pressed two of his fingers over Michael's open lip and the pain and swelling instantly faded as the wound closed. The older man then touched Michael's back where he had felt pain when raising his sword earlier. That sharp pain too faded, leaving only a memory of an ache in its wake.

"You should be much better come morning. Now, get plenty of rest, and please be careful the next time you encounter that monster. I don't have much strength left for healing, especially anything too complex. Thank you for coming here to deal with our problem. I'm sorry that other knight came and interrupted your fight with the beast," Yoska said as the glowing in his hand subsided.

"Will there be any scars left from this?" Michael asked.

"Only in your ego if you let those types of scars remain. Your lip will have a mark for some time, but that too shall fade," Yoska assured.

With his business concluded, the elder motioned toward the door with a slight bow, and Michael took his cue to leave the hut. He returned to the Chubby Owl and, after removing his armor and weapons, climbed back into the surprisingly comfortable bed, and drifted off to sleep.

Chapter Five

Michael carefully worked his way up into the trio of mountains north of Haran. Thinking of them as mountains still didn't sit quite right with him, especially after his time living in Feldring. Granted, he hadn't lived in Feldring in…three years, so he could have been misremembering the mountain city that was his hometown. Still, he watched where he was stepping and ensured he had good footing before making any drastic movements. He did, after all, have to be careful not to make too much noise, lest the manticore hears him and attack before he was ready. He didn't even know where the beast was, except that it flew in the direction of these mountains. That was at least helpful to know.

He had formed a plan for taking on the manticore. He would set a trap for it, wait where the monster couldn't see or smell him since its sense of smell was something to be concerned about, and wait for the trap to spring before he attacked. It was a crude plan if calling it a plan at all was even accurate, but it was better than waltzing up to the monster and attacking wildly.

Michael knew painfully little of the manticore species. Its size alone was daunting. He also knew it flew toward the mountains. And it was minorly injured. He could use all of these facts to track the beast to its home, which he assumed was some cave here in the mountains. Additionally, based on what the villagers had told him, the manticore had been taking their livestock. And it hadn't been successful in taking any of the cows in a few days, so the monster was likely hungry. This told him it would be aggressive and, he hoped, careless. When Týr got aggressive in fights he sometimes got reckless, forgetting tactics, and simply striking wildly when he found an opening. Generally, that worked for him, but Týr was a former thief and he fought differently than a hungry monster.

Working his way through the rocky exterior of the mountains, Michael found himself wishing he had gone on a few more hunts with some of the other knights. Not the knight he had met the previous evening. Or had it been early that morning? Regardless, the only hunting he had done since being knighted was for a few deer, and only once had he been successful. That hunting was for food, and he realized that was different than trophy hunting. Not that he wanted a trophy from killing the manticore. He just knew there wasn't a purpose to this hunt beyond saving the village of Haran and the kingdom's supply of cattle.

Michael walked with his bow out and an arrow nocked on the string, ready for whatever may come his way. The only things he could see though were rocks, small patches of some kind of green plant he had never seen before, and more rocks.

Soon, he crested the smaller of the three mountains and could survey the area around him while he continued his search for the elusive creature. The mountains seemed manually created rather than occurring in a more natural means. There were only three of them, and each of them was more or less separated from the others by a trench that resembled passes. The mountain formation was odd as well. There were two mountains together, both of which stood to the north of the smallest and most southern mountain, where he stood.

Looking across the expanse to the next closest mountain, Michael saw part of the mountain flattened and had what appeared to be a large cave in the side. That could be a good place to check for the manticore. From where he stood, reaching the cave would require him climbing a nearly sheer cliff face, something he hadn't prepared to do. He had neither the equipment nor the desire for that. Climbing up the cliff would also leave him exposed to the manticore. It would have no difficulties picking him off the cliff and simply dropping him if it so chose.

Rocks nearby tumbled down the side of the mountain and Michael turned sharply to his left to see what the source of the noise was. He was surprised to find the other knight casually walking toward him.

Chapter Six

I figured I would find you out here," she said, approaching cautiously, seeing that Michael had his bow partially drawn. "I don't wish you any harm, Sir Michael. I am here to help."

"I doubt I need your help," Michael replied. "I think the manticore is over there." He pointed to what he thought was a cave on the other mountain. This earned him a nod from the other knight.

"My name is Sela, by the way. Lady Sela the Gentle, Knight-Commander."

"You certainly don't punch gently," Michael joked, motioning at his face. He had examined his face in the mirror that morning when he was getting ready for his excursion and saw that, while the wound had healed, there was still a bruise that had formed and a faint scar that remained. He had prepared for that, as Yoska had warned him about the potential for scars.

"Teaming up on this fight will be better than either of us trying to take on such a monster alone," Sela suggested.

"That makes sense," Michael acquiesced after some thought. "Where do you think this thing is hiding?"

"The cave you pointed out earlier is certainly a possibility. But the manticore will want to have a good view of the surrounding area so it can watch for prey and approach as it wishes. If it is truly among these mountains, there's a good chance we have already been spotted and are being stalked as we speak," Sela stated.

"What do you suggest in that case?"

Before Sela could answer, the sound of large wings flapping caught the attention of both knights who turned and found the manticore circling overhead, drawing closer with each pass it made. They had stood around too long and now the beast had found them, catching them by surprise.

Chapter Seven

"Give me your bow!" Sela shouted.

Michael handed her the bow with the arrow still nocked, and she drew the arrow back, touching the tip of her thumb to the corner of her mouth before releasing the arrow into the sky. The arrow sailed toward the manticore and struck its target, though it was hard to tell where. The only tell that the beast was struck at all was the roar it let out, which sounded pained rather than angry.

The manticore, making another circle, closed its wings and dropped toward the pair of knights on the ground. As it approached, the monster opened its wings again and caught itself, landing as gracefully as such a large beast could. It roared and flapped its wings at the knights, pushing them around with the air.

Michael drew his sword, and out of the corner of his eye, he saw Sela gently set down his bow and draw her weapon. Instead of a sword, it was a mace, though it was on a shorter haft than was common for such a weapon. *How had I missed her having that?* he scolded himself for not noticing things about the other knight.

Together, the knights squared up against the manticore. Michael felt uncertain about what role he would play in this fight, as they hadn't discussed any plans before they got ambushed by the monster. That was when Michael noticed that the manticore was simply watching them, eyeing both knights as if it were trying to figure out which of them presented the biggest threat to it.

And that's when the manticore attacked, using its front paws to swipe at the knights. Sela dodges the first strike and brought her mace down on the other paw when it approached, catching it in the air. The beast reeled back and howled, shaking its paw. It then brought the same paw downward, attempting to crush Sela under its foot. She rolled back to avoid the attack and when she had recovered, she brought her mace down on the beast once again.

Michael rotated to the side of the monster and jumped toward it, swinging his sword over his head, and connecting with the manticore's front left leg, slicing through its thick hide, and exposing the muscles and tendons that made up its elbow. The beast roared and swiped at Michael, who ducked beneath the giant paw that came his way. He stepped back and prepared for another attack.

Before he could ready his sword, the manticore crouched and its tail flashed, piercing Sela right through her abdomen. The tail wasn't even slowed down going through her steel cuirass or back-plate. It lifted the knight and slammed her into the ground. Michael rushed and swung his sword, slicing right through the thick, scaly tail. When his sword sliced through, the tail snapped back, and the manticore shrieked before it jumped into the air and flew off, leaving splatters of blood on the ground behind it.

Michael dropped his sword and dropped to his knees at Sela's side, trying to help her. She resisted his help, batting his hands away from the still pulsing tail that seemed to have pinned her to the ground. Michael stopped trying to help and sat back on his feet, surveying this situation. He didn't know what to do, and at a time like this, that terrified him. Should he try to save his fellow knight from what seemed almost certain death, or chase after the manticore now that it was wounded and would leave a trail wherever it ended up going?

"Michael, leave me. I am no good to anyone right now. Even if we get this tail out of me, I can't fight. Go bring down that bastard!" Sela begged through obvious agony.

"I can't leave you here. What if it comes back to finish what it started?"

"It won't. Go, chase that thing down. You almost have it. Without its tail, it's no different than a lion with wings. And it's bleeding. Badly," Sela stated, her voice now faint and breathy. Michael had to focus to hear what she was saying.

"I can get you back to Haran. It's about an hour's walk from here. Just let me help you stay alive," Michael begged.

With a trembling hand, Sela reached under her cuirass and removed a ring worn on a chain. It was her signet ring! Michael stared, confused about what was happening. With a forceful tug, she broke the necklace and placed the ring in Michael's hand, closing his fingers around it. Michael opened his hand and examined the ring. It was a simple gold band with a flat top where a rabbit was carved into the stamping surface.

"Take this. Show it to Orson and let him know I helped as best I could. I'm sorry about last night. I know you more than earned your knighthood. I just got upset and lost my temper needlessly. Now, leave me and kill the manticore," Sela requested again.

Michael tucked the signet ring into the money pouch on his belt, stood up, and retrieved his sword from where it had landed. He returned the sword to the scabbard hanging from his left hip and examined the ground around him for the trail of blood that the manticore had left behind.

Chapter Eight

The trail of blood left by the manticore was easy to follow. Every meter or so there was a splotch of dark goo mixed with some green substance that Michael assumed to be poison. In his mind, it made sense that the manticore would have a poisonous tail. He wished he had had more time to prepare for this endeavor, he found himself thinking as he found another splatter of blood on the ground. Having time to speak with Joshua or some of the other Mages about the manticore would have been beyond helpful.

Eventually, after climbing back down the mountain he had been on, Michael found a large pool of blood the manticore left on the ground, likely from its landing. There was a smear in the blood and poison as if it had landed then swished its tail. The beast had to be weakened from its wound, and Michael found himself hoping this would make the next fight with the monster easier.

Upon further examination, Michael found a cave and noticed the blood smear led in that direction. This was not where he had thought the monster would be when he had been on top of the mountain, but he was glad to know his suspicions about a cave were correct. Perhaps he would put together a field guide, after all of this was finished, detailing his findings of the manticore. Some of the other knights would likely find such a thing useful. He would consult with Joshua about that when he returned to Shemont to see how he should go about doing that. He had never written a field guide before, and the thought of doing so scared him a bit.

One thing that scared him more than the thought of writing a field guide about the manticore was fighting it. He was alone now and while he had located the monster, he still had to fight it. And worse than that, he had to survive. He had no idea what its weak spots were, where it would be most vulnerable to his attacks, but he had to push on for the king and especially for Sela, who was counting on him.

Michael approached the cave he found where the trail of blood went. He was hoping to find the manticore inside and finish this fight. He had no torches, and while there was still some light, the sunlight would fade quickly in the mountains. He had to hurry. Everything pivoted on his ability to kill this monster. Without hesitating any longer, Michael entered the cave and immediately heard the beast somewhere within.

Chapter Nine

The sound was the most unsettling thing about the cave, which was nice and open. It seemed to be a series of caves that all branched off the main tunnel. He didn't have time to check every offshoot for the manticore, but he was able to follow the sound at least. It grew louder as he went deeper into the cave. Pained breathing filled the cave and thankfully drowned out the sounds of his footsteps. The hard soles of his boots would have echoed too much in the cave, but he was thankful that he could move somewhat silently, under the cover of the animal's labored breathing.

Just as Michael thanked the Allfather for the covering sounds, everything in the cave grew deathly silent. And as he had suspected, his boots rang out against the stone, echoing his location for the manticore to easily find him. Everything about this plan seemed to be unraveling before it had even started.

Movement.

Michael stopped dead in his tracks and drew his sword and shield. He could hear something faint, almost undetectable. But it was certainly there. It sounded like the manticore was approaching, it's giant paws whispering on the ground as it moved somewhere in the cave.

Suddenly the monster roared, which echoed through the cave, bouncing off all the walls of hard stone. Michael was paralyzed by the noise and found himself instantly overtaken by the monster. It rushed at him and while the beast did run past him, he was still in shock from the noise when it finally turned around and pounced. Michael moved out of the way of the pounce, but only just. Despite its injury, the monster was still faster than he wished.

The manticore moved its front right paw and tried to sway Michael, but it missed somehow. Michael swung his sword and struck the beast, earning another ear-shattering roar. He nearly had to cover his ears from the noise being so loud. But he was, barely, able to manage. While the monster was still roaring, Michael pivoted so he was standing underneath its great frame, its belly exposed. With a quick motion, he brought his sword across the beast's soft middle and moved out of the way of more blood as it gushed from the new wound.

The manticore yelped and lunged back, knocking Michael to the ground as it moved. He had just enough time to stand up before the other pay came flying at him. This time, he brought his sword straight for the large lion's mitt, catching it in the air, between the two center toes. The webbing between the claws sliced cleanly and another howl of pain echoed through the cave. This time, Michael ignored the pain in his ears and swung his sword for the beast's face, though he missed.

Michael prepared himself for another attack against the wounded creature but had to back off as it tried to strike at him again. He had to raise his shield to protect himself from the massive claws. Unfortunately, he hadn't thought about how strong those claws would be and they cut right through his shield and his leather bracer. He felt warmth on his arm and knew he was bleeding, though he couldn't stop and assess how badly he had been hurt. He had to keep fighting.

Once again, the beast pounced at him. After barely dodging this, Michael found himself under the monster as it tried to find him. Wanting to end the fight, Michael thrust his sword upward; the blade glided easily between two of the manticore's ribs and the monster heaved forward. He yanked his blade free from its chest and stepped to the side, swinging his sword, and catching the hind leg as the monster fell to the ground. Blood gushed from the wound in its chest and stomach, as well as from its tail.

Michael stopped and panted, catching his breath as the manticore lay on the floor of the cave, wheezing and coughing blood. Seeing this, he felt a sense of remorse for causing a living thing this much anguish. He knew it was a necessity, as it had threatened the peace and safety of the village. Additionally,

Michael reasoned that this was an apex predator, and as such, he couldn't let it live only to recover and attack again. He would be saving lives by ending this one. Weren't many lives worth more than just one? Michael shuddered at the thoughts of justifying *not* killing the monster.

His line of reasoning finished and over, Michael cautiously stepped toward the dying manticore still lying on the ground. Keeping an eye on the massive paws and accompanying talons, Michael approached the head. As he drew closer, the manticore locked eyes with him, something he hadn't expected. What he had anticipated even less was how oddly…human the eyes seemed. They were a golden brown, even in the dying light that seeped into the cave from outside. So many emotions flooded those near-human eyes. Fear was one of them. That threw Michael for a loop. How could such a ferocious monster be afraid of him? Wasn't it supposed to bring fear to those who saw it, rather than the other way around?

Starting to feel pity for the creature again, Michael took a deep breath and plunged the blade of his sword, point first, into the monster's neck until the tip of his sword struck the stone on the other side, then pulled the sword toward him and freed the blade from the fur-covered gullet. Blood and air poured from the monster's throat and Michael stepped back to avoid getting any on his boots. It was silly, he thought, to protect the leather of his boots from such a mess. They were leather boots after all. They would clean, and he knew that much. It was still out of some unknown habit that he tried to keep his boots clean.

Chapter Ten

Michael carried the severed head of the manticore, the proof of his accomplished deed, toward the village of Haran. He had managed to find his way back to where Sela had been before he chased after the wounded manticore, but she was no longer where he had left her. He kept wondering where she would have gone, injured in the manner that she had been. The only logical conclusion he could come up with is that she had been gathered up by one of the villagers and taken back for some emergency healing.

As Michael approached the village, he saw that a crowd was starting to gather, wanting to see the triumphant hero's return from the hunt. While the sun had already dropped beyond the western horizon, the villagers were easy to see based on the torches they were carrying. Yoska was the only villager not holding a torch, other than a few children he saw in the crowd, instead opting for a small crystalline light placed that emitted from the top of his stave. The light was soft and white, yet still was brighter than most of the torches combined.

Now that he was finally close enough to the villagers, Michael set down the manticore's head and rested his hands on his knees, panting from having carried the heavy thing for a few kilometers. Yoska approached, looked over the kill-proof that Michael provided, and nodded deeply. He reached toward his belt and removed a pouch that jingled with coins. Michael didn't bother inspecting the contents. He was satisfied just knowing that his job was finished and that he didn't have to think about that look he had gotten from the manticore right before killing it.

"How's Sela doing?" Michael asked. His question was received by a blank stare. "The other knight. How is she?

"We haven't seen her since we asked her to leave the village," Yoska replied.

"Give me a torch," Michael demanded. He grabbed the presented torch a bit roughly and ran back toward the mountain. He knew he had to find her before it was too late.

Within half an hour, Michael found his way back to the spot where he had last seen Sela and found a trail of blood different than the one left by the manticore. This trail went up toward the mountain's peak, which wasn't far from where they had fought the beast side by side. Michael followed the trail and, as he had suspected, found Sela leaning against a boulder that hadn't managed to roll down the mountain.

She was still. Her chest wasn't even moving with her breathing. Michael knelt beside his fellow knight, removed his left gauntlet, and placed two fingers against the side of her neck. Nothing. He had been too late. Had taken too long. He had failed her. All his hard work had been for nothing. Sela had died without knowing that the manticore had died and that Michael had once again earned his title as a knight. That was something he had been looking to prove to himself more than anyone else.

With nothing else he could do, Michael removed the manticore's tail from her stomach. He then stood and picked up Sela, gently carrying her body back down the mountain and toward Haran. He hadn't been a knight long, but one thing he had done was study the traditions of knighthood and how Drendil honored their fallen warriors. Especially those who fell in battle. He would give her a proper warrior's funeral: a pyre set alight at the darkest time of night. By his estimation, it would be about another hour, which gave him plenty of time to prepare the pyre.

When it was finally ready, Yoska and a few other villagers had gathered to help with lighting the fire. Following the traditional ceremony, four torches were to be used, one at each corner. Villagers had already doused the wood with oil so the fire would burn brightly, again as dictated by tradition. The first torch was set to the oil-soaked wood, then the next three followed in quick succession. As expected, the pyre burned brilliantly, lighting up the area around it as Sela was sent home to the Allfather the way all fallen warriors were. After staying a respectful amount of time, Yoska and the other villagers departed, returning to their homes.

Michael stayed until the only thing that remained was ashes and the steel plater armor that she had been wearing, which was now blackened by soot and ash. Reverently, Michael gathered the armor, which would be returned to the castle's armorer to be forged once again, this time into something stronger, more significant. As he grabbed the last piece of armor, Sela's winged helmet, he breathed a quick prayer for her soul, asking that the Allfather guide her back home.

Murder

Chapter One

The late evening air was warm and beyond humid, but in Shemont, that was common during the summer months. After the sun dropped beyond the western horizon, Sir Michael the Valiant walked down the cobblestone road outside his estate, heading toward The Dwarven Cave, a tavern he frequented that also happened to be close to his estate. While he didn't consider himself a regular there, the innkeeper knew what he liked to drink and usually gave him a free ale or two. Especially after the ordeal with the manticore, Michael found himself frequenting the tavern more than before. It was still difficult for him, knowing that he could have saved Sela's life, had she not refused his help.

Michael opened the door to the Cave, the shorthand name he called the tavern, and was instantly greeted with the strong smell of tobacco smoke and spilled beer that had soaked into the straw scattered on the floor. Michael enjoyed the smell, the environment, the dark wood of the bar, and the sound of scraping chairs against the floor. He felt safe and welcome here, a place he could relax and be himself. It was a place where people didn't ask too many questions besides the occasional "How was your day?" a question Michael usually answered if he felt like it.

Once inside the tavern, Michael found an open stool at the bar and sat down then waited for the innkeeper to come over with a beer. Frank was a good man and treated his customers well when they deserved it. Short and stocky, he built the floor behind the counter to be higher than the rest of the tavern so he could reach the end of the bar when needed for wiping down the occasional spill, or grabbing an unruly customer by their collar before the one guard that worked in the tavern came over and shoved the person through the door. Michael had only seen that sort of exchange happen once, and, after watching the way Frank handled the situation, he wasn't surprised that it was a rare occurrence at the Cave.

Frank waddled over and placed a mug in front of Michael, frothy foam nearly flowing over the top. Michael accepted and reached for his coin purse to pay the man for his delicious ale, but Frank waved and shook his head vigorously, though he said nothing. Michael knew the routine by this point but still insisted on reaching for his coin purse. After frequenting the Cave enough, Frank knew that Michael was always good for what he owed.

Michael picked up the mug of ale, brought the metal cup to his mouth and tipped it back, gulping as much as he could handle. The ale itself, auburn with a cream-colored foam, was cool and went down smoothly. The little bubbles tickled as they went down his throat, but that was a welcome sensation and one that he looked for when drinking beer. The flavor was almost flowery, with a hint of sweetness, like a spring morning. Both those elements together helped the beer go down quickly, and within a few minutes, Michael found himself needing another, which Frank promptly provided.

As Michael watched the innkeeper fill his tankard again, Michael let his mind wander. It immediately took him to the village of Haran where, not long ago, he had been setting up a funeral pyre for a knight he only just met. Sela. She fought valiantly against the manticore, but despite their efforts, the beast took her life. This haunted Michael still. He hadn't been there when she died, but he ensured she received the honors she was deserved as a knight of the kingdom. He still wore her signet ring, a simple gold band with a rabbit engraved on the flat face, on a chain around his neck. The ring would serve as a reminder to him that sometimes there was nothing that could be done. Sometimes, all you could do was accept a loss.

His second beer went down quickly, though a touch slower than the first. Frank once again came over with a pitcher and filled the tankard, ensuring Michael wasn't waiting too long with an empty cup. This time, Frank poured a touch too zealously and the foam spilled over the edge, sliding down Michael's hand as he sat at the bar considering the turns his life took in the past few years. There was too much loss in the past three and a half years since he had left his home city of Feldring, far away in the land of Prikea. Beyond the sea.

Týr. Svenka. Sela. All acquaintances. All gone. There was nothing he could do but pray to the Allfather that their souls were safely harbored into the afterlife. Each of them was taken from his life by Vor'Kath or one of the monsters he brought into this realm. Each of them was a casualty in this great war against chaos. Against the Madness. Each of them deserved the sweet revenge of Vor'Kath's death. Only after that would Michael begin to feel better, he thought. Vengeance. That is what helped to push him forward each day.

Michael's third beer disappeared just as quickly as the previous one. He waved Frank away when he came by with the pitcher, not quite wanting a refill yet. He wanted food. Frank always made really good food. *Maybe some roasted lamb would help me feel better*, Michael thought. He considered this for a moment longer then waved Frank over. The innkeeper finished refilling another patron's tankard then filled Michael's for a fourth time, despite the false protest that Michael gave toward the matter.

"Lad, you look grim tonight. Still thinking of Sela?" Frank asked, his gruff voice somehow comforting. Michael always thought the man sounded like a handful of gravel being thrown against a window.

"I could have saved her," Michael stated, confirming the innkeeper's rightly placed suspicions.

"How about some food, lad. That always seems to cheer you up. I have a few different dishes tonight. Lamb and vegetable stew, lamb chops, or pork steak with onions. The chops and the steaks will both come with roasted potatoes and some vegetable or another. I have no idea what all Rosie's cooking back there, but I do know it's those three things," Frank admitted. The dishes he described all sounded so good.

"How's the lamb tonight?" Michael asked.

"It'll cheer you right up, lad. Tender and juicy with some kind of new green stuff to spread on the meat. It's made from mint, and before you go giving me that look, give it a try. I promise it'll fix your mood right up," Frank promised.

"I'll take the lamb then, Frank."

"Good. Rosie will bring it right out for you," Frank said before he whistled at one of the tavern maids as she made her rounds. Getting a series of waves and gestures from Frank, the girl walked into the kitchen, at the back of the room. She returned a brief moment later with a plate and brought it over to Michael.

As Frank promised, the plate bore three lamb chops, a heap of roasted potatoes, a green vegetable that Michael thought looked like small spears, and a small dish with some gelatinous glob of green stuff. Michael picked up the small dish and sniffed, catching the undeniable scent of mint just as Frank said. Figuring it couldn't hurt anything to try, Michael put a touch of the green stuff on his first lamb chop and set to work cutting the tender meat from the bone. The bones all came free with minimal effort, leaving Michael with three hearty chunks of roasted lamb, which he eagerly started eating.

The mint concoction added an interesting new flavor to the lamb, though Michael found he preferred the meat without the extra stuff. Each bite he took was better than the previous. Juice dripped from the meat as he cut new pieces from the bigger chunk and the meat was so tender that he barely had to use a knife, though he still did simply in the name of easy eating.

Right as Michael started working on the last piece of meat, he heard a commotion outside the tavern, though he ignored the sounds. It was likely some minor street brawl that the guards could handle. They were usually bored on quiet nights and secretly wished some kind of action would happen, and Michael didn't want any of the guards on patrol to be disappointed.

Michael briefly stopped eating and took a drink of beer, enjoying the taste of everything together when he heard a scream that chilled him to the bone. Hearing the scream, he slammed his tankard down, dropped the fork from his other hand, and rushed out the door.

Chapter Two

There in the middle of the street, he found a ghastly sight. A woman lying on the street, blood splashed all around her. Her abdomen had been ripped open by something, there was no sign of what had done this, and her throat was ravaged as well. Michael rushed over, kneeling beside the woman, and placing his hand on her neck to check for any signs of life. Nothing. She must have let out her scream moments before her attacker struck her throat.

Taking a quick look around, Michael saw pawprints in the blood and a trail that went down the street, heading east. He quickly got up and followed the tracks until they faded not far from where the woman now lay in the street. He looked for any further signs of the killer, checking high and low, but saw nothing. It was a cold trail. *Damn!* he thought angrily to himself.

When Michael turned around and started to return to the murdered woman, a guard ran around the corner, his sword in one hand and a torch in the other. Seeing Michael, he brandished the sword and ordered Michael to stop moving, raise his hands, and drop to his knees.

"I didn't do this, Sergeant!" Michael shouted back at the man, who was taken aback by his knowledge of the army's rank structure. Not many knew how to tell differently ranked soldiers apart unless they bore a crested helmet.

"Sir Michael, is that you? I thought this was the Cave but didn't know for sure," the man said, holding the torch higher above his head and getting a better look at Michael. He quickly returned his sword to its scabbard, seeing that Michael wasn't a threat.

"I was eating dinner when I heard the scream. Rushed out here and she was dead. I tried to follow these tracks," Michael said, pointing out the pawprints in the blood, "but they lead nowhere. They stop right over there."

"Those tracks look like they came from a big hound," the guard said. Michael looked closer and sure enough, they did. The prints were roughly the size of Michael's hand. The beast had to be big to leave those.

"This doesn't look good. Any idea what would leave these?" Michael asked. The guard said nothing, but instead shook his head and shrugged his shoulders.

"Would you mind helping us find out what happened here?" the guard requested eagerly. "We don't have the manpower on the streets for something like this. It seems more within your line of work."

"I can help with this. I just have a feeling *I* will need some help with this—"

Chapter Three

What kind of help?" the guard asked.

"Do you know where Joshua lives?" Michael inquired.

"I can go get him right quick. Don't let anyone else touch the body while I'm gone," the guard requested before running off in the same direction as the pawprints.

Michael knelt beside the body again and examined the markings left in the flesh. He saw deep gouges that were likely left by impossibly wicked fangs. Where the fang marks were found, Michael saw something else that concerned him. Charred flesh. It was as if the attacker was made of fire or used some kind of fire Magic in addition to biting the victim. There also appeared to be multiple sets of fangs, as none of them all made the same markings in the victim's flesh. Some of the fangs were longer than others, leaving deeper tracks. Others were shallower and pointed slightly outward, something the other set didn't seem to do. This was very puzzling.

As Michael stood, he noticed people were starting to gather around the scene, whispering their concerns and trying to get a good look at the body. Michael disliked this, knowing that rumors were often detrimental to an investigation. But before he could say anything to the crowd, the sergeant and Joshua came running around the corner. The guard made a cacophony of noises as his armor rattled and his boots clicked against the cobblestone streets. Joshua, by contrast, made hardly any noise with his robes and slippers.

"Alright, everyone. I know this is strange and you all want to rubberneck and form your ideas as to what happened but get back inside. Things might get more dangerous before all this is said and done," the guard requested of the crowd that formed. No one left, though many stirred or shuffled their feet.

The guard started to bark another order but before he could a bright flash of light and a loud *bang* sounded above the crowd and everyone scattered. Michael felt the hairs on the back of his neck stand up and instantly knew someone cast a spell. That was one of the gifts he had, thanks to his sensitivity to Magic. He couldn't cast any spells himself, but he could tell when one was cast. Confused, the guard looked up then to Joshua who grinned, having been the one who cast the spell.

"Sometimes, a little touch of Magic is all that's needed to motivate people. Now, what do we have here?" Joshua asked, looking at the body on the ground.

Michael ran through his findings from the pawprints on the cobblestone to the differing marks in the victim's body. Joshua stopped and stared at his comrade after hearing that detail. His face drained of all color and his eyes widened as far as they could.

"Is there any chance these are claw marks instead of another set of fangs? You only pointed out one set of pawprints…" Joshua mentioned before his voice cut off sharply.

"I don't understand your concern, Sir Joshua. Are you suggesting this was one creature?" the guard asked.

"That's exactly what I'm suggesting. That's the only thing that would make sense—"

"*That* is what makes sense? How would there be more than one set of fangs on a single animal? I swear sometimes you Mages—" the guard started before he promptly shut his mouth.

"Not finishing that sentence was the best idea you've had tonight, Sergeant," Joshua noted. "Now, I have an idea of what we are dealing with here, but I need to make sure."

Joshua immediately cast a spell and started investigating the area. The spell was like a window, but when you looked through the surface, it showed a faint trail of blue-grey smoke rising from the ground that went in the same direction as the pawprints. Joshua started following the trail and Michael followed, not wanting to leave the Mage alone. Thankfully, the sergeant stayed with the body.

Chapter Four

"What are you seeing?" Michael asked, unsure of what was going on.

"This is what I was expecting. We aren't dealing with a wild animal, Michael. Magic is involved. This is something far worse than either of us could have expected," Joshua replied.

They reached the end of the bloody pawprints and the trail of Magic kept going, though it grew weaker beyond the end of the physical evidence. The trail of Magic continued for almost a block before it faded, showing no signs of the creature. Michael looked around, hoping it wouldn't ambush them in the street, but saw nothing.

"Michael let's go back to the body. Show me everything that you've seen that stands out as strange to you," Joshua requested.

They went back, and Michael showed the charring on the skin and the different impressions made by what he suspected were different sets of fangs. Upon closer examination, the throat also contained different marks than the abdomen did. The markings indicated fangs that seemed to point inward and down, and there were the same charring marks he noted before.

"Does this monster have three mouths?" Michael asked, hoping the answer would be no. He also prayed that the other two hadn't stepped in *any* of the blood or left any other traces that they had been present at all.

"From what I remember," Joshua said, "yes it does."

"What is this thing we're dealing with," the guardsman asked.

"I have to go to the Battlemages' library quick. They have a book I was studying two days ago, and thought was interesting but slightly useless. What a fool I can be at times," Joshua scoffed at himself.

Joshua stood and opened a portal well away from the crime scene, attempting to preserve what little evidence they possessed. He stepped through and the portal snapped shut. When the spell ended, Michael felt the hair on his neck lay down once again.

"He does that often?" the guard asked.

"What, go through portals?" Michael returned.

"Yeah. That is so concerning, I don't know how you can—" the guard started when another portal opened, and he was cut off.

"This isn't good, Michael," Joshua said, stepping through the portal with his face buried in a small, leather-bound book with yellowed pages.

"What is it?" the guard asked.

"Read these two pages. I believe this is what we're dealing with," Joshua stated, handing the book to Michael who started reading aloud.

"…Hellhounds are ferocious beasts shaped like canines but created of fire or other elements. While they often travel in packs and are controlled by demons, see the section on demons, this is not always the case. Because they are elemental creatures, they can come in any shape and size and may have one, two, or more heads. Commonly, these beasts are found to have a trio of heads and attack anything they see at will. Use extreme caution when dealing with these monsters, as they will not relent until their quarry is dead…"

"Allfather save us," the guard breathed.

"What does this mean, Joshua?" Michael asked. "We're dealing with a demon dog made of fire?"

"That's exactly what this means. I suspected when you showed me two sets of fang marks and only one set of pawprints but seeing the Magic residue and the charred skin around these bite marks confirms it for me," Joshua stated.

"That book says they're sometimes controlled by demons. Can we kill the demon controlling it and make the hellhound go away?" the guard asked.

"That's a great idea, Sergeant. One fairly big problem with that plan is: where is this demon?" Joshua asked.

"What is our next step?" Michael asked.

Chapter Five

Come with me, Michael," Joshua requested as he opened another portal. The two knights stepped through and the portal closed behind them.

On the other side of the portal rose a massive white-stone tower with windows placed in various spots. Several outlying buildings sat around the tower, connected by small pathways of the same stone. A series of fires, each burning a different color, lit the pathways. Michael could see the same colors he saw in most sunsets or sunrises, but there were other colors, like black, white, and green as well.

The knights walked toward the tower and as he approached, walking up the long staircase, the doors appeared to open on their own. Joshua walked in first and Michael followed.

Inside the tower, everything was pristinely white except a simple wooden desk where someone in white robes sat with a ledger, a quill, and an inkwell. The man sitting behind the desk appeared to be maybe seventeen years old. Michael never asked Joshua how old he was, but he knew that using Magic obscured a Mage's true age.

"Good evening, gentlemen. I'm sorry but the College is closed for the night. You are welcome to come back tomorrow—" the Mage behind the desk started when Joshua cut him off.

"We are here from Shemont where there has just been a gristly murder. I believe it was done by a hellhound," Joshua started, getting a wildly concerned look from the man at the desk. "Who should we speak to about this matter?"

"That would be Master Kerron, but I don't know if he's in right now. Should I go retrieve him or would you like to get him yourself—"

"Please retrieve him," Joshua said.

The man behind the desk stood, cast a portal, and vanished through the shimmering doorway in the air. A moment later, the young man returned with another Mage following him. The other Mage was an Elf of shorter stature than most Elves Michael previously met. His pointed ears stuck out to the sides, rather than the points going back. Like the man sitting at the desk, the Elf also wore pristine, white robes, but the cuffs of his sleeves showed a rainbow of stripes, each stripe the same size except the black, which was slightly larger. Michael knew there was something significant about the colors but didn't want to ask a foolish question right now. There were other, more pressing matters at hand than what the colors meant.

"Gentlemen, I hope there is truly an emergency going on in Shemont, as this pupil has told me. I would hate to have been woken up for nothing—" the elf started when Joshua cut him off.

"A woman was killed by a hellhound," he stated curtly.

"How can you be sure?" the Elf asked. Joshua explained all the clues that Michael found, and the Elf's eyes grew wide. "Allfather let this be false!"

"I'm afraid it's true, Master Kerron. We need your help to find and put down this monster and maybe even the demon that controls it," Joshua requested solemnly.

"Show me the spell you used to track the Magic residue. I might have a different one for you to use. Tracking a hellhound is not going to be easy work for either of you. Please use caution dealing with this monster and its demon master," Kerron implored.

Joshua quickly cast the spell he used in the street and Kerron nodded, then cast his own version while he walked Joshua through the process. Joshua nodded then tried the spell, getting the same window spell that the Elf created. Seeing this, Master Kerron nodded approvingly, then bid his farewell to the two knights.

"Thank you for the assistance, Master Kerron," Joshua said, bowing slightly. The Elf did not reciprocate the bow. Instead, he turned, opened a portal, and left the lobby area of the tower.

Chapter Six

Once Master Kerron left, Joshua and Michael left the tower. Joshua didn't wait for them to get down the stairs before he opened a portal back to Shemont, right outside the Cave. Michael's stomach grumbled, and he thought longingly to the food that awaited him at the Cave. He cleared the thought from his mind and focused on the task at hand. He needed to find the hellhound and its master, dispose of them both, and only then could he worry about dinner and a good night's rest.

The street was still empty except for the dead woman and the guard watching over her. In their absence, the guard procured a white linen sheet and draped it over the body. Blood soaked through the plain white blanket, leaving perhaps a more gruesome sight than just the body.

Joshua told the guard to remove the sheet from the body, then cast the spell Kerron showed him. With the window spell open, he inspected the bite and claw marks left in the woman's flesh from the attack. Looking over Joshua's shoulder at the body, Michael saw tendrils of red-brown smoke rising from the markings and wondered what the strange smoke meant. Before he could ask, Joshua turned toward the pawprints left in the blood and walked the same trail they followed before.

Joshua stopped dead along the trail and looked around quickly. Michael, not sure what else to do, drew his sword, ready for whatever caused his friend to look so concerned. Joshua turned toward Michael at the sound of his sword releasing from its scabbard and shook his head. Michael was premature in removing his sword, but he would rather have it out in case it was needed. He found himself caught off-guard one too many times in the past and wouldn't make that same mistake again.

Chapter Seven

Are you seeing this, Michael?" Joshua asked, pointing at a spot on the cobblestone street. Without looking through the window spell that Joshua was casting, Michael saw nothing out of the ordinary. Then he looked through the spell and saw what his friend was seeing. Pawprints. Lots of them. If he had to guess, Michael would have said there were at least a half dozen sets of prints left on the ground, glowing red-hot against the cobblestone.

"What does it mean?" Michael asked, unsure of what he was seeing.

"I don't know; this is new. I would imagine they are close, but I don't know for sure. Keep an eye out for anything out of the ordinary," Joshua warned, his voice strained slightly.

Michael immediately began examining their surroundings. They were walking down a slightly wide street with no crossing alleyways or side streets. In this environment, it would be hard for the demon and his horde of hellhounds to ambush them. That at least was reassuring, but Michael wasn't completely confident in his ability to read battlegrounds when fighting elemental specters or their immortal masters. He never fought a monster that wasn't an organic creature before. Something about this terrified him to his core.

Chapter Eight

At that moment, Michael looked down the street and noticed several figures stalking toward them. One walked upright on two legs, but it was far from human. Given the midnight colored skin, wicked horns, and face that glowed with fire, Michael knew it must be the demon. In its right hand, it carried a nightmarish, fiery axe. In its left hand, the demon held half a dozen chains, each connected to what Michael immediately knew to be the hellhounds.

While they resembled dogs, as the book had described, they were far from being ordinary dogs. Each one boasted multiple heads. Each head snarled and snapped, wanting to be let free of the leashes. Every beast had spines jutting from their backs and wicked tails that snapped back and forth, leaving trails of fire behind them. Their faces glowed with the same fire as the demon's, and a light glowed from within their bellies. They lurched forward, pulling at the chains that bound them to their master. The hellhounds were all large, roughly the size of a mountain lion. Because of their multiple heads, the beasts all had a much wider chest than a cougar would, and their front legs were spread wider than the back, their shoulders extended to compensate for their extra necks. Of the hellhounds, all but two had three heads. The remaining two only boasted a pair of snarling, slobbering faces that Michael knew lusted for blood. As if they hadn't already consumed enough this night.

His sword still drawn, Michael stepped out from behind Joshua and approached the demon and his monstrous minions. *How do you even kill a hellhound?* Michael thought to himself, hoping his sword would be enough. As he approached, the demon released the chains from its left hand and they instantly vanished, allowing the hellhounds to charge at full speed toward Michael and Joshua. Three of them closed the fifteen-meter space between themselves and the knights far quicker than Michael expected from such large beasts. The other three stayed behind, likely scheming or preparing to ambush if he was overwhelmed by the first three. He hadn't read enough of the book Joshua grabbed to know how they would fight, but that seemed like an obvious tactic to him. Let the first three tire him out and attack when he was weakened or overrun

As the hounds approached, Michael entered a defensive stance, his sword held with the blade forward so he could easily bring the weapon down through whichever monster approached him. The first of the hellhounds leaped, its fangs and claws ready to be buried in his flesh. With a quick motion, Michael brought his sword down through the center head, slicing it cleanly in half before he stepped to his left to get away from the falling monster. The other two heads whimpered, and the hound retreated, while the two others still approached just as quickly

The second beast approached but ran past him, trying to get around and behind. Michael spun and brought his sword up, the blade slicing through its middle. The fire that glowed inside the monster burst forth in a flash of light. Michael turned away to keep his eyes properly adjusted to the night.

The first hellhound lurched forward again, this time from his left, at the same time as the third and Michael jumped backward, avoiding the snapping of five sets of jaws. The two creatures, thrown off by his dodge, ran into each other and they fell to the ground together into a heap of what Michael now saw wasn't fur but instead seemed to be scales that resembled dark stones. *What are these things?* he thought. The hounds, merely stunned from the impact, struggled to regain their footing.

Another of the hellhounds, one of the three that stayed behind, leaped over the two that were standing after their collision. Michael had just enough time to duck, as he felt an intense heat pass over him as the monstrosity came within centimeters of touching him. As Michael stood, the fourth hellhound's tail whipped, and he felt a scorching sting flash across his back as the fiery tip of its tail dug into him like a bullwhip. The pain overwhelmed him, and he stifled the urge to cry out.

The two dogs on the ground before him were finally on their feet, and Michael brought his sword across, from right to left, cutting through the remaining heads. The one that had been cut through before dangled limply and nearly dragged on the ground. Both beasts fell to the ground and crumbled away, leaving only piles of dark ashes behind. Three hounds remained.

He turned to face the one that jumped over him and found the monster was no longer there. Instead, it leapt onto the side of a building and started running back toward its master. Michael stepped forward, approaching his enemies. One of these dogs had three heads and the other two only had two.

One of the two-headed dogs circled to Michael's right, the other to his left. He knew they were trying to get him in a pincher movement, and he knew how to counter that when fighting men. Beasts from another dimension were entirely different. The dog on his right lunged, and a moment later he heard the one on his left do the same. With both dogs in the air, Michael stepped forward and spun around, his sword flashing through the swampy summer air. While his sword missed both dogs, they didn't miss each other, colliding just as the others before. These dogs recovered more quickly though, and sprung forward, their maws opening as time seemed to slow down. Michael could see the fire glowing inside their mouths, and the only thing he could do was move to his left and try to avoid the monsters entirely.

As he moved to his left, the third dog met him, who had been circling him the entire time, staying carefully out of Michael's line of sight. With no opportunity to move out of the way, Michael caught the third dog on his arm. All three mouths clamped down, piercing his leather armor as if it wasn't even there. Their mouths were smoldering, and Michael let out a cry of agony as the dog yanked him to the ground. As he fell, his sword dropped from his right hand and clattered against the cobblestone. The beast snarled as all three mouths tried to tear at his arm. The other dogs approached his feet, but Michael kicked them frantically, and they backed away.

He quickly assessed the situation and threw his right hand into the middle dog's snout as it released his arm to bite again. The dog caught the full brunt of his fist and the other two mouths released, the pain somehow affecting all three heads. This gave Michael just enough time to grab his sword and stand before the other two dogs attacked once again.

Before Michael could react to any of the dogs around him, three bolts of lightning dropped from the cloudless sky, one connecting with the dog that bit him. The other two managed to avoid the strikes. The stench of smoldering flesh filled the air as another bolt of lightning consumed the fourth hellhound. With a quick look, Michael confirmed this dog also dissolved into a pile of ashes.

Michael, taking the opportunity handed to him, brought his sword downward, slicing through the chest of the fifth dog. The severed body spewed fire from the wound instead of blood. Once again, Michael turned his head away to avoid losing any of his night sight, but he was too late. The flash lit up the street and blinded Michael, who staggered at the brightness of the light.

At that moment, Michael heard a familiar *twang* sound coming from further down the street. An arrow with large white plumes sailed through the air toward the final dog. Michael watched the arrow as it flew and then bounced off the dog's stiff, rocky hide. There was no time to turn and see who fired arrows at the beast. He had to strike fast.

His left arm wounded, Michael used all the strength in his good arm to thrust his sword into the dog's chest, feeling heavy resistance as the blade met the thick hide. Still, the blade penetrated the dog, slicing right through its heart and lungs. The dog whined and dropped to the ground, another flash of bright light coming from its decaying body as Michael withdrew his sword from its chest. Once again, he found himself blinded by the flash of light, but he knew the fight was over. There were no remaining hellhounds.

Chapter Nine

As Michael stepped around him to fight the hellhounds, Joshua closed the spell he opened. He prepared a couple of other spells to fight the demon, expecting a tough fight. In his left hand he held frost and in his right he held lightning. Either on their own should overwhelm the demon. Together, it would have to hope for a miracle to save itself.

The hellhounds lunged at Michael and the demon flashed forward, raising its smoldering axe over its head as Joshua threw his first spell, a bolt of lightning, right into the demon's belly. The creature writhed and stepped back but seemed otherwise unaffected by the spell. The axe came down, but Joshua stepped to the side, casting his frost spell which coated the demon in ice. Joshua stepped back. Joshua prepared two more frost spells.

The demon shook and the ice broke free around it. It vanished again, and Joshua quickly spun around, hoping to find the bastard soon. The air shimmered. It…moved. Joshua could see nothing, but clearly, something was there. He heard the chains the demon used to contain the dogs. They jingled in the air somewhere nearby. Another flash and the demon reappeared, less than a meter away.

Joshua barely got out of the way of the axe, thrusting both hands forward and encasing the demon in ice once again. He stepped back and to the left, circling the frozen specter. Another spell. More frost. This time, instead of a stream of icy cold, he formed a spear made of ice. He plunged the spear into the demon's exposed side. The monster rippled and howled, a deafening sound unlike anything Joshua ever heard before. The ice shook free from its wounded body and the demon vanished again. Joshua scanned the air around him, looking for the shimmers he saw before.

A flash of blinding light materialized close to Michael as one of the hellhounds disappeared. Joshua closed his eyes and turned, but the light was still too intense. He opened his eyes again and the demon was back, its axe once again raised over its shoulder. The thing's fiery face opened like a chasm. Joshua stepped forward and thrust his hand forward, casting another bolt of lightning, once again in the monster's belly. It reeled and vanished again before reappearing on the left a meter away.

Behind the demon, Joshua could see Michael now had only three of the hellhounds left. The hounds circled the other knight, and Joshua watched as two formed a pinching formation around his friend, while the third hung back, out of sight. The Mage hoped his friend would notice their plan of attack and be able to effectively combat it. Joshua returned his attention to the demon before him just as the axe swung from one side to the other.

Joshua dodged backward and once again thrust his hand toward the demon, but this time it was prepared for him. He felt the chains wrap around his arm, the heat coming from them piercing his robes instantly. The demon pulled Joshua closer, grabbed him by the throat, and raised him off his feet. The demon was tall and built rather large. Joshua felt the thing's hand tighten around his throat and he grabbed the fingers that gripped him by the neck. With what little he could do, he cast a spell and the demon's hand froze. The contrast between its smoldering hand and the icy spell was unsettling, but the demon released him and stepped back.

Michael screamed, the anguished cry cutting through the noise of snarls and growls. One of the hounds had him. The demon approached Joshua. Quickly, Joshua cast a spell he used a few times before, once while he battled a sea serpent on his way to Drendil, years ago. It took a second to cast the spell, but lightning dropped from the cloudless sky, one bolt catching one of the hellhounds, another catching the demon as it raised its axe once again. The bolt surged through the axe and into the demon, jolting its entire body. It staggered and spasmed as residual lightning coursed through its body.

Before the specter could recover, Joshua formed another icy spear and rammed it through the demon's head, nearly splitting its face in half. The body writhed and contorted, and the axe fell to the ground where it shattered before entirely disintegrating. Joshua removed the spear of ice and the demon collapsed in on itself, leaving nothing behind.

Another flash of light signaled the end of the final hellhound, and Joshua bent forward, his hands on his knees as he panted, recovering from the fight with the demon. It had been a while since he fought that hard all the while casting such demanding spells so quickly. He gasped until he finally recovered his breath.

Chapter Ten

Michael turned and saw Joshua doubled over and gasping as he recovered from his fight. With the fight over, Michael turned his attention to his arm, bleeding and throbbing with an agonizing intensity. He could still feel the heat of the hellhound's mouths on his arm.

Michael walked over to Joshua, returning his sword to its scabbard as he did so. When he was close enough, he reached his right arm under the Mage's left, and helped him stand fully upright. They walked briefly like this before Joshua stopped and motioned for Michael to turn. The Mage's hands started to glow with a warm white light as he covered the wounds in Michael's arm. The throbbing pain subsided and the heat stopped momentarily. His arm no longer felt wet and sticky from the blood. When Joshua removed his hands, Michael inspected his arm and found no reminder of the wound except the holes in his armor. *The damn beast ruined my armor*, Michael thought angrily.

"Can't imagine the castle armorer is going to be happy with me," he chuckled as he showed his friend the damage.

Michael and Joshua returned to the body lying in the street. A man knelt beside the body uncontrollably sobbing. By the simple gold ring on his left hand, Michael assumed him to be the husband of this poor woman. Michael stepped beside the man, knelt, and placed his right hand on the man's heaving shoulder. The man sobbed for a moment before rudely brushing Michael's hand away.

"I don't need any damn comforting. My wife has just been killed," he said without looking at Michael. "Leave me to grieve."

"We have just killed the monsters that did this to her," Michael said.

"What good have you done? She is no less dead now than she was an hour ago," the man growled in response. Michael could see the muscles in his jaw clenched as he said this.

"We have brought justice to this tragic end," Michael said, attempting to comfort the man.

"Thank you. I shall take my justice home and put it to bed for the evening. What good is *justice* when my *wife* is dead?"

"I'm sorry for your loss. We will let you grieve in peace," Joshua stated, grabbing Michael by the shoulder, and pulling him from the sobbing widower. They walked away from the scene, leaving the sergeant with the man kneeling beside his wife's body.

"We did what we could, Michael. There is nothing left for us to do here," Joshua said once they walked from earshot of the man.

"Why can't he see that?" Michael asked.

"Michael, you should be more sensitive toward him at a time like this. Not every soul that we cross is going to be thankful for what we do. We can do nothing more for him," Joshua stated. "Now, go home and get some rest. You will need to sleep after the healing I gave you. Tell George I said hello when you get back."

Michael nodded and walked toward his estate, feeling all the fatigue from the fight suddenly set in. As he walked, his mind wandered, taking him back to Haran where he said good-bye to a fellow knight he had barely known. He thought of the man crying in the street right now. It seemed unfair that life treated these people so poorly, yet he knew there was nothing to do about either situation. Joshua was right, they did all they could. Sometimes, there was nothing more to do beyond that.

The Basilisk

Chapter One

Sunlight beat down on the ground and reflected off the endless sand. Sweat. Beads gathered on his forehead before trickling down his face and stinging his eyes. There was nothing he could do about that right now. He had more pressing matters. He needed to get out of the sun, but the vast unnamed desert on the eastern side of the Ash Mountains offered him no shade. There was simply nothing out here. Tales of old told of monsters that inhabited the ruins within this expanse, yet he saw nothing except the infinite dunes. They were likely just tales, but he wanted to check the rumors of monsters. Some were said to be so fierce they could "turn a man to stone with just their eyes." That one seemed far-fetched. How could something petrify a man with eye contact?

Though he doubted there was any truth behind the rumors, Michael trudged on through the scalding sand. Hills formed as the wind blew the grains of irritating particles across the surface of this vast nothingness. Having never been in a desert before, Michael found himself surprised by how the sand moved with such fluidity and grace. The hot, dry wind pushed against what little exposed skin he had. The sand danced as the air forced itself over the ground and toward the mountains that rose to the west. Swirls of sand grains stood and frolicked as Michael walked through the vastness of the desert.

Rumors always pointed to there being something at the center of this sea of nothingness. Michael intended to find the source, be it treasure, monsters, or empty ruins. He *would* get to the bottom of the rumors.

The ground rumbled, sending strong vibrations ran through his boots, trembling every fiber of his being. These tremors only lasted a moment, yet everything stopped. Michael froze, his hand snapped to the hilt of his sword, and he waited for whatever had been moving through the ground. He had never experienced anything so massive like that, and he hoped he never would again. From the last few years, he had spent studying the bestiary of Drendil, he knew it *couldn't* have been anything alive that made those vibrations. Perhaps he had missed something in his studies?

Once the tremors subsided, Michael moved forward, pushing toward what he hoped would be the center of the desert. His hand released the hilt of his sword and he felt the tension ebbing as he took a few more steps. Periodically, he reached for the simple necklace he wore, a gift from Joshua. The Mage seemed more than concerned about this endeavor and gave Michael the necklace as a way to ensure his safety. The token was his only companion out here in the desert. His trusty gelding, Watson, remained in the stables outside Shemont, as there was no reason to risk the horse's life out here in the desert. Michael stopped the moment that thought passed through his head. His horse was more important to him than his own life.

Still, curiosity gripped him when he heard the rumors. He would find the crumb of truth he found existed in tales out here among the dunes and blazing sunlight. Surely, something existed out here.

Chapter Two

Far away, in the safety of the library at the Sorcerers' College, Joshua lounged at a table with a stack of books sitting before him. Six books sat in a stack, and another three books sat before him open to various pages. He scoured through their age-stained, yellow leaves and looked for anything that would help Michael. Joshua considered this a somewhat pointless expedition into the desert, but he still agreed to help because Michael was a good friend. How could anyone say no to a good friend?

Joshua already had a day of studying in the library planned when Michael approached with his grand idea of adventuring into the desert. The major change in Joshua's day was what he studied.

Instead of researching spells, he read about the desert. He perused the books looking for any relevant data that he could find. He sought a few things specifically: the desert's name, any previous civilizations that may have lived out there, and any creatures known to live in the sand. One book covered fauna, another flora. One book outlined the otherwise forgotten history of Drendil. Joshua loved history and looked forward to that book in particular. That would be his reward for finding the rest of what he sought.

As he opened another book, this one about the desert fauna, a thought pestered at the back of Joshua's mind. Michael wandered through the desert, battling the elements, while he sat here in the library safe from everything but excessive amounts of dust. He knew Michael would be fine, so long as nothing overly aggressive or hostile lived in the desert, but the thought still bothered him. Skimming through the table of contents, Joshua found a chapter dedicated to the desert, but he still could not find the blasted name for the desert. He flipped to that section of the book and started skimming through the pages. Spiders with hair, scorpions, a variety of snakes, and lizards all lived in the desert. Joshua found none of those were aggressive and he felt himself calming down until he flipped to the next page.

"A basilisk," he read. He had never heard of that creature before but after reading the page, his heart pounded so violently, it felt like it was coming through his ribs. A lump formed in his throat and his stomach lurched, threatening to relieve him of the food he ate a few hours before.

Quickly, he inhaled through his nose and held the breath for a few seconds until he felt his heart start to speed up then released the breath. He repeated this a few more times until the pounding of his heart slowed. He closed his eyes, set the book down on the table, and took himself to the void in his mind where serenity alone existed. He discarded all other emotions. He had learned this technique as a young boy on his journey to priesthood.

Joshua opened his eyes and read the page about the basilisk again, this time going through the details carefully. The creature seemed to be a hybrid of a lizard and some kind of fowl. It sported glands under its jaw that would secrete a venom toxic enough to paralyze a man in seconds. The author noted that the basilisk would either have two or four legs, each one ending in eagle-like talons used to tear the paralyzed prey to pieces before feeding. Nothing within these two pages told whether the monster existed.

He set the book down. Something this bizarre would be known by someone. Surely, a lizard-bird hybrid could not exist without someone seeing it somewhere. Reading the books would no longer be enough. He needed help. If the basilisk was real, Michael was in danger.

Chapter Three

The sun dropped behind the mountains and the relentless heat dissipated from the sandy desert floor. Michael thanked the Allfather for the relief and removed the scarf from his face that had kept the sun from blistering his skin. Without wearing the scarf in the sun's presence, the heat washed over his exposed skin, and beads of sweat became rivers that flowed down his face. This is how he imagined an oven felt to a chicken roasting inside.

Using both hands, he reached to his sides and undid the clasp that held the pieces of his leather cuirass to the backplate and removed the burden of his armor. No longer warmed by the sun and radiating sand, the wind carried a tinge of chill that he found welcome. Under his armor, he wore a thin linen shirt just to keep his armor from making direct contact with his skin. The shirt dripped with the sweat it collected throughout the day. Between the wet shirt and the cool wind, he shivered and felt his skin tighten and prickle into small bumps he didn't expect to have in the desert.

Now unburdened by his armor, Michael removed a small, folded piece of parchment from a pouch on his belt. Once unfolded, the paper revealed a map he had scrawled before Joshua opened the portal for him. Rough drawn, the map showed the major landmarks he needed to navigate the desert. He oriented himself to the map and surveyed his surroundings. The Ash Mountains stood leagues behind him, and in the distance, before him, he could just make out the Gilded Ocean in the dying light. Standing atop a dune gave him a good vantage point, but the light faded now that the sun was behind the mountains.

According to the map, the Gilded Ocean surrounded him and this sea of nothingness and sand. From the rumors Michael heard, something existed in the desert close to the eastern coast. He looked east and thought he could see something in what little light remained. Looking harder, a structure rose from the sand and it wasn't another dune. Whatever it was, Michael knew he had to investigate it. He judged the distance from where he stood to the structure and guessed it was another league away, something he could cross in an hour of hard pushing. He quickly put away the map, threw his leather armor on, and set off once again, keeping his eyes pointed in the direction of the something he saw in the distance.

He descended down the dune and into deep, loose sand that rose past his ankles. This slowed him down; walking through it was weird. Some areas of the desert varied in how the sand behaved under his feet. In some areas, he could walk as usual on the surface, and in others, each step felt like agony as his feet sank almost to his knees in the sand.

Michael paused with sand up to his ankles and removed his water flask from his belt and took a deep draught. The water was still warm from the sun. Hot water without tea leaves always tasted strange to him, but he needed the water after walking through the desert during the hottest part of the day. After taking a drink and replacing his water, Michael put his armor back on and set off for the structure rising from the sea of sand to the east.

Chapter Four

As he suspected, it took a little more than an hour to reach the structure. Getting closer to it, Michael was able to get a better picture of the thing. It was not a massive structure, as it had appeared from far off. A large boxy shape, the entire thing reminded Michael of a mausoleum. At what he assumed was the front stood an open entrance; it resembled a courtyard. A series of three pillars stood on both sides of the doorway and supported an overhang about five meters from the ground. Three shallow, platformed steps led from the sand to the doorway.

From standing outside, Michael saw no light anywhere around or inside the structure. Inside, even less light existed as the sun finished setting when Michael approached. Without any wood, he couldn't make a torch for light. This was problematic, but not the end of the world. He simply would have to make do with what he had with him.

Something skittered and sand rustled behind him. The grains tumbled over each other as something flashed across the surface. The blade of his sword whispered against its scabbard. Moonlight flashed across the polished steel. He turned, ready for whatever was behind him. He felt the nodules in the hilt of his sword as they dug into the palm of his hand. The leather wrapping protected his hands slightly, but while the nodules looked pretty, they did hurt at times. His right foot came back behind his left foot and planted in the sand. He spun to his right, his left foot pivoting on the ball and he snapped his head to see…nothing. He was alone in the desert. Somehow this reality sat poorly with him.

His stomach ached and his heart fluttered. His hands trembled and shook, and the moonlight reflecting off his sword danced in his peripheral. Michael took a deep breath in and let out a long sigh. He longed for some action, but it seemed nothing worthy of a fight lived among the grains of sand. Perhaps the rumors about the petrifying beast came from people's fear more than any stretch of reality. Michael returned his sword to the scabbard and turned back toward the structure. He looked up from the sand and saw…

Chapter Five

Michael didn't know what to call this thing. It was a large lizard, but with bird-like features. It had bright green, yellow, and red scales that covered its entire body and a pale belly with, what he imagined, were softer scales. Red eyes shone in the bright moonlit sky. Four legs carried it off the sand and each foot showed three digits. Each digit boasted a razor-like talon. The thing's back carried a crest of feathers that ran from just behind its head to near the end of its tail. These feathers were a bright turquoise and showed oblong yellow spots that resembled eyes on the ends. Under its jaw, placed on either side, Michael saw two bulges that pulsed as the creature snapped its jaw at the air. It bobbed its head back and forth, as it examined Michael for the brief moment that passed where he couldn't move. It *had* paralyzed him. He would have to confirm that part of the rumors when he got back to Shemont…*if* he got back that was.

Michael could hear the beast breathing, could see its chest expand and collapse as it inhaled and exhaled. It waited for something. Why didn't it attack when he could do nothing? He wasn't expecting to see a monster behind him and now, seeing one, his legs each weighed hundreds of kilograms. Lead blocks replaced his feet and he felt unable to move. His arms hung at his sides, dead to any signals passed to them from his brain. He screamed inside his mind to draw his sword, but nothing happened despite all his inner shouting.

Just as Michael yelled inside his head to grab his sword, the lizard stood on its back feet and flared its feathers toward him, mesmerizing him. With its prey distracted by the display, it sprang from the sand toward him. This was the moment that his feet decided to obey their commands and he stepped backward. He barely avoided the beast as it crashed into the sand with a *thud* that shook the ground.

While the monster recovered from hitting the sand, Michael drew his sword from its scabbard, hearing the scrape of the steel blade as it came free. The lizard swiped at Michael with its front left foot and the talons came within a hair of touching Michael's armor. He didn't doubt they were sharp enough to cut through the thick, stiffened leather. He imagined they would make quick work of his flesh too, given the opportunity.

Not wanting the lizard to have any more opportunities to strike him, Michael switched his tactic and went on the offensive. His lungs emptied with a furious shout that echoed off the nearby structure. In the same instant, he started swinging his sword back and forth, attempting to scare the creature. This tactic seemed to work as the beast crouched under the swinging sword and backed away, quickly, from the man who lost all sense that he once had.

Focused on his offensive strategy, Michael paid little attention to his foe's actions. He saw it moving away, nothing else. He took a step toward the lizard-bird, and as he recovered from one swing of his sword noticed it moved to the side, trying to get around him. He pivoted and brought the sword down in the direction of the beast. The sword missed the body, but he did trim a few of the flapping feathers, the pieces floating down to the sandy desert floor. The monster reeled and backed off again, lunging without warning. Michael tried to dodge again, but this time he wasn't fast enough, and he felt the talons slice through his right arm just above and below the elbow. Searing pain shot to his shoulder and pinched his neck. It felt like the muscles on his right side pulled tight. He quickly switched his sword into his left hand and regretted not doing more training with that hand. He was right-handed, but as a knight and a warrior, it was a good idea to practice with both hands for instances such as these.

The lizard darted past Michael as he awkwardly raised his sword with his left hand. He turned and watched as the creature scurried into the structure, its feathered tail vanishing into the dark opening. Michael walked back to the structure. His arm now burned and throbbed. Besides, when he fought the hellhounds and got bit by one of those nasties, Michael hadn't felt anything this intense before. Dizzy. Sleepy. Sluggish. He had to push on but more than anything he wanted to lay down and sleep off the pain in his arm. He dared not to look at the wound or it would feel worse.

Michael approached the structure and put his foot on the first of the platform stairs leading into the opening. As he stepped up, a new wave of dizziness crashed through him and he stumbled backward, falling into the sand. His arm stung when it touched the grit-covered ground. Without thinking, Michael looked at his arm and regretted that choice. The pain intensified with just the sight of the wound. He saw three simple scratches on his arm, but something about them seemed rather strange. For one thing, he could see what he assumed was bone in each of the cuts. He also saw something bubbling along the edges of each wound. Seeing the wound, he saw the edges of his vision starting to grow dark and shook his head to fight off the blackness.

This seemed to work, and he stood up, ready to make his way into the structure after the lizard creature. He got to the second platform after a few sluggish steps, and it took far too much energy to pick his foot up to reach the next level to get into the mausoleum. Another wave of pain. Dizziness. A blackness that threatened to blind him. He couldn't go on. He had to sit and rest. *What's happening to me?* he thought. His internal voice sounded distorted. Distant. Detached. Wrong. He knew, somewhere in his mind, that he shouldn't sit down and rest. The pain was too great. Another wave of agony washed over him as he stood there debating with himself. He needed help and soon. Joshua was supposed to be standing by to help him. He just had to…touch the…necklace…

Chapter Six

If I understand you correctly, the basilisk *is* real but can't petrify a man with its gaze alone," Joshua stated. This seemed so contradictory from what the fauna book had said. Granted, that book seemed exaggerated in more aspects than just that tidbit.

"Correct. The basilisk cannot *literally* petrify a man with its eyes. The term petrify was a mistranslation from the old Elven word for paralyze, which is a—" the librarian started when Joshua cut him off.

"I don't have time for an etymological discussion right now. A man is in that desert right now looking for the basilisk, and he is only going off rumors of what the thing is. You said it's nocturnal and likely to let its prey suffer before feeding. What can you tell me about where it might live?" Joshua asked, trying to keep his voice level and calm. It *mostly* worked.

"I would imagine it would live in the ruins there, but I can't say for sure…Hey, do you hear something buzzing?" the librarian asked. More than a touch of curiosity filled his voice. Joshua darted back to the table to see the raven trinket rattling on the table, the light no longer glowing. Michael was in trouble.

"Where are those ruins?" he asked, turning to the librarian who arrived at the table with all the books Joshua had checked out.

"Well, there aren't exact maps of them, but…"

"Where are they! My friend's life is in danger!" Joshua barked, spooking the librarian and a few other Mages in the room who looked up to see why there was a ruckus.

"Hey, keep your voice down," one of the others barked.

"It's fine. Please go back to your books," the librarian assured.

"Where are the ruins?" Joshua asked, purposely keeping his voice quiet yet firm. Already startled from Joshua's surprise visit to the library, the squatty curator adjusted his spectacles with a trembling hand.

"They're near the coast. If your friend is in trouble, we need to send someone to…"

"I'm the someone we are sending. Now, who can make me a portal as close to those ruins as we can get?"

"Oh, do you not know the spell for portals? I can teach you if you—"

"I know how to make portals. I've never been there before and can't imagine the place in my mind," Joshua explained.

"Right. I sometimes forget that rule. Let me go find someone who could—"

"From the Ash Mountains how long would it take to get to the ruins?"

"Well, that depends on how—" the librarian started to say then noticed the look that formed on Joshua's face. He cleared his throat and changed what he was going to say, "A little under two hours."

Joshua snatched the raven trinket off the table, apologized for not being able to return his books to their shelves, opened a portal to where he had last seen Michael, then stepped through into the desert.

Chapter Seven

Joshua pushed through the sandy terrain while he kept an eye on the raven. The light no longer glowed from somewhere deep inside the crystal. Instead, it pulsed every few seconds. That was part of the spell he had cast. If Michael moved the raven would glow, but if Joshua moved the raven would pulse. It also gave him the general direction he needed to find Michael. He prayed to the Allfather, loudly in his head, that he got there in time. One thing he certainly trusted from the fauna book was that the venom worked fast after a basilisk attack. He could think of a few reasons why Michael would have stopped moving. His primary concern was an injury. Even if that turned out not to be the case, he would rather tread on the side of safety than having a friend die under his watch. *You should have been out here with Michael instead of hiding in the library*, he scolded himself as he ran across the sandy surface of the desert.

The raven continued flashing as it pointed Joshua toward the sea. A different part of it would flash depending on the direction that he held the trinket, it was currently flashing toward the head and beak. The placement of the light within the trinket would move as Michael did, providing Joshua with rough directions. Though limited in its application, it proved to be a useful spell.

Joshua crested a dune and stopped, panting as he caught his breath. In the distance, he could see a structure, and just as the librarian said, it was near the coast. He didn't have much further to go. He hoped Michael was alright though he felt a pit forming in his gut that told him he was walking into a potential disaster.

Chapter Eight

Joshua tried to keep track of the time that passed as he made his way to the structure. There was no doubt that Michael was there because as he drew closer the raven trinket pointed directly at the structure. He guessed it had taken a little over an hour for him to arrive at the structure, though telling time while running in the sand was difficult. He stopped thrice on his way to catch his breath. Running was something he despised, and the sand made the journey that much worse. He had tried to keep his mind off the agony in his legs, pressure in his chest, and the abundance of sand that managed to find its way into his shoes. He could only ignore so much before he had to stop running.

He approached the structure and saw Michael sitting with his back against a wall, sword on the ground in front of him, and blood forming a puddle around him as it dripped from his arm. A set of three gashes marked his arm and upon further examination, the wounds showed signs of infection and sand that gotten into the openings. He would need drastic attention soon. At best he might lose the arm. At worst, his life.

Joshua prepared a healing spell he learned long ago that would remove infections from a wound. He had to stop its spread, at the very least, before it reached Michael's heart. Joshua formed the spell and pushed it toward Michael but heard something move on the sand before the spell could touch the wounds. He quickly set the spell, anchored it, and turned around and saw the same creature depicted in the fauna book. The basilisk. *Where did it come from?* Joshua thought to himself. He had scanned the area before he approached the structure and had seen nothing.

He expected the basilisk to be bigger, seeing it now. It was roughly three meters from head to tail. Its legs were about a meter long and had pronounced joints that bent its powerful-looking limbs to mask its true size. The beast stood in the sand and swayed back and forth, its jaw snapping as it sized up its new prey. Joshua stood as still as he could, hoping it would leave after a few minutes if he did nothing to threaten it. He hated having to kill something that may be the only member of its species. It had hurt Michael though, and he couldn't risk it hurting any other adventurers who came out here in search of whatever treasure was rumored to exist in this forsaken desert.

Instead of waiting for the beast to make the first move, Joshua cast a series of spells at the basilisk and stepped away from Michael to avoid causing any more harm to his already injured friend. Fire and lightning flashed across the sand as the basilisk showed its true speed. Joshua swore to himself and cast another spell at the monster as it dashed here and there and jumped onto the pillars that supported the overhanging roof.

He continued casting spells, each of which missed the basilisk as it kept moving. Several minutes passed where Joshua continued casting spells only for them to miss the basilisk. After a few more bouts of spells missed the creature, Joshua stopped casting, feeling himself growing weary. He needed to save some of his energy so he could heal Michael from his wounds. The basilisk saw this as an opportunity and lunged toward Joshua.

Fangs. The beast's open maw approached quickly. Joshua could see venom dripping from the ends of its sharp, elongated teeth. His opportunity was fading. He had one chance at this. With his left hand, he threw a wall of air and his right threw a bolt of lightning stronger than any he had cast before. He watched as the stiff air blast from his first spell contacted the monster and it sailed backward toward the sand. *Clap.* The air crackled as the wall of air broke around the beast which caught the bolt of lightning as it touched the ground. Scales flew from the basilisk as the lightning surged through its body. An ear-shattering shriek echoed off the dunes and the ruins. The air took on a strong smell, a mixture between burning flesh and the coming of rain. The mixture of smells sickened him; his stomach started to lurch as both smells hit him together.

The basilisk lay still on the ground, smoke rising from various places where scales had popped off from the lightning. Joshua held two spells, ready for the moment the beast moved again. He watched it for what felt like an eternity. He released his spells when he was satisfied that it was dead.

No longer holding the spells, his joints ached, muscles cried out, and his legs buckled, dumping him onto the ground on his hands and knees. When he inhaled, a wheezing sound followed, and he started coughing before recovering a few minutes later. It had been some time since the last spell-casting fight he participated in, and as he stood, he felt out of practice as a combative Mage. He switched gears and turned to Michael who was still sitting on the ground. More blood had joined the pool that formed under him and his skin was pale. He had lost so much blood. This would not be easy healing, and Joshua was still weary from the fight with the basilisk.

Chapter Nine

Kneeling beside Michael, Joshua assessed the situation as thoroughly as he could. His heart was still beating, but what should have been the beating of a drum was now the occasional blip of water dripping from a leaf after a heavy rain passed through a forest. The venom from the basilisk's claws no longer infected the wounds, but he still had to clean the sand from the gouges. In his mind, he prioritized everything and steeled himself for the tough journey ahead.

Joshua formed a water spell that would flush the sand and other debris from the wounds. If Michael remained anywhere near consciousness, everyone within earshot would know the instant this spell touched his arm. Joshua gradually lowered the ball of flowing water onto his friend's wounds and braced for the inevitable cry of agony that should have emitted from the man. Nothing. This was far more serious than he had assessed. He pushed more air into the water orb to further flush the wounds and watched as countless grains of sand broke free. They swirled through the water; specks of dirt caught in a whirlwind infinitely larger than they were. Joshua found it entertaining but wished he could experience this under any other set of circumstances than this.

As the water flushed the wound and freed the trapped sand, it also dissolved whatever clotting had already started in the wounds when the blood mixed with the air and dirt. The orb of water quickly turned red as fresh blood poured into the liquid. Joshua understood the body's natural healing process from his training to be a priest. While every priest was a Mage, typically most only ended up using simple healing spells to bring about the Allfather's will. Priests, when asked, cured common ailments like infections as well as reversing cuts and broken bones. Something that simple was often just using spells to speed up the body's healing process.

To heal Michael, Joshua had to take his time, walk through everything properly, and most importantly he had to fight to bring the man back from the brink of death. His heart was still pumping blood, which Joshua counted as a blessing. It was struggling, but it was still beating. He was thankful for that much. This situation could have been worse.

Joshua released the water spell and the orb of water splashed on the ground, creating a sickening *splat* as the water and the blood mixed. He ignored the sound and continued working on closing Michael's wounds. The sky started growing lighter by the time he finished the entire process. Joshua had closed the wounds and had returned fluids to Michael's body with the hope that it would help speed his recovery process.

Though he was still unconscious, Michael would wake up in his own time. His pulse was strong again. It was a beat on a small drum, but it was more regular than it once was. Scars would remain from this ordeal, and Joshua hoped those scars would serve as a reminder not to chase rumors.

Trying to stand, Joshua found himself light-headed and overwhelmed by the fatigue that had plagued him since the fight. He placed his hands in his lap and started meditating, the only thing he knew that would relieve him of the tension and aching that surged through his body. As he cleared his mind, he teetered and fell onto his side, consumed by the post-battle weariness.

Minotaur

Chapter One

The door creaked on its poorly oiled hinges as Sir Michael the Valiant left the guardhouse at the end of his shift. As he walked down the stairs, the boards creaking beneath his boots, he looked around and saw the same thing he always saw at the end of his shifts: the smiling faces and sidelong glances that people feared he saw. He could hardly go anywhere without someone recognizing him as a Hero of the Siege. Michael didn't feel as though he truly warranted such admiration for his knighthood, but that was out of his hands. All he could do now was strive to be worthy of the title and fame that accompanied it.

The sun had long since started its daily descent toward the western horizon, bathing buildings in the city with a faint pink hue as it crept closer toward its destination. This was Michael's favorite time of the day because everything calmed down as the evening grew longer. No longer did he hear the cries of the merchants as he passed through the market. No longer did he need to make his way through crowds of market-goers, only to feel uncomfortable as they parted around him in awe.

He made his way through the nearly empty streets, passing buildings constructed with stone at the base and wood and plaster on top. The white plaster glowed pink in the late evening sun and Michael found himself enjoying the scenery of the city even more. Shemont was a truly beautiful city, even if it didn't have the intricacies found in Anselin. Granted, Magic coursed through the very bones of the Elven city, something that showed in every aspect of their architecture.

Michael turned down a street and stopped outside a quaint tavern he frequented called the Dwarven Cave. The innkeeper, Frank, would likely have kept Michael's favorite stool available for him in case he stopped by after finishing his day's duties.

Michael disliked many things about his life at the moment. Guard duty was growing monotonous, especially since he only oversaw the patrols instead of walking the streets. The most exciting part of his day often remained a stop in the Cave, as the regulars called it, for a pint or two on his way home. The Cave rarely had a dull night and he counted on that to break up the unchanging cycles of life in which he felt trapped.

As he opened the door to the Cave, a small bell overhead dinged, announcing his arrival. Frank turned toward the door and grinned at Michael as the knight moved toward the end of the bar. Straw covered the wooden floor of the dimly lit tavern. Behind the bar, Frank waddled over, grabbing an urn of fresh beer, and pouring a mugful for Michael as he sat atop his favorite stool. Michael took a deep drink from the tankard, appreciating every sip as the perfectly chilled beer hit the back of his throat. He set down the tankard and greeted Frank as he always did, getting a toothy grin in response. It had taken some time for Michael to adjust to that smile, but now he knew that's just the way Frank was.

"How was your day, Michael?"

He appreciated that Frank was one of the few people in his life that dropped the 'Sir' from his name. The status of being a knight brought its privileges, some he expected and others he hadn't, but too often people saw him as more than he was. At the core, he was a person, just the same as everyone else. Nothing about him really changed since he left Prikea all those years ago. Sure, he wielded a sword now and he wore the livery of a Captain in the Drendillian army, but besides those things, very little about his life was different.

"It was just another day, Frank. What's Rosie cooking today?"

"Venison stew, same as last night. You want any of that?"

"I think I'll fare better with whatever George is cooking. No offense meant toward Rosie, of course," Michael added.

"Ah, I won't tell her you said that. You're in the clear, lad."

"Can I get a top-off?"

Frank poured beer to the top of the tankard. "Certainly."

"Thanks."

Michael took another drink from the metal tankard, something Frank didn't provide many of his patrons in the Cave. Most of the tankards were wood; their handles and brims were worn smooth after untold years of use. As he sat on his stool and drank, Michael removed his pipe from the pouch on his belt where he kept it and the cherry-flavored tobacco. He carefully filled the pipe the way that Master Gamel had taught him years ago. He started with a tightly packed layer that just covered the bottom of the bowl followed by a fairly tight ball of tobacco that he pushed into the bowl. Lastly, he sprinkled some loose leaves on top before striking a match and lighting the pipe. He puffed a few times as he held the match over the bowl then blew the smoke toward the ceiling. Frank brought over an ashtray and placed it next to Michael's drink on the bar.

Michael grabbed his tankard and drank from it once more, savoring the sweet aroma and flavor of the beer as he drank it. The slight taste of cherry in the tobacco accompanied the beer perfectly, just as it always had. He sat at the bar and puffed on his pipe, drinking from the tankard occasionally between puffs. Very little could ruin such a great end to a long day of listening to guards reporting the status of their patrols.

As Frank filled Michael's tankard again the bell above the door rang, announcing someone's arrival. Michael paid little attention to the ringing of the bell, though, as he rarely met anyone here. The other soldiers in the tavern stopped their drinking and snapped to their feet. It was with that cue that Michael turned to see Master General Alwin standing in the doorway, looking around. He quickly set down his pipe and stood as quickly as he could before the man's eyes rested on him. The Master General smiled and nodded slightly seeing Michael, obviously not surprised to see him.

Alwin motioned for the soldiers to take their seats then walked up to the bar and grabbed a tankard that Frank placed in front of him. He took a long drink then looked at Michael, wiping the foam from his lips.

"The king needs to see you about an assignment. I stopped by your manor and George said you'd most likely be here."

"Can I finish my pipe first?" Michael asked with a sly smile.

"Of course. I won't ruin a man's pipe even for an assignment," the General chuckled.

Chapter Two

Welcome, Sir Michael. I'm glad that Alwin was able to find you."

"He mentioned that you have an assignment for me, sire."

"Right to the point. I knew there was a reason I picked you for this, Sir Michael. Someone sighted a Minotaur in the woods between the Sorcerer's College and Anselin. Neither Erkan nor I have the time or resources to send patrols into the woods to verify this account. I need you to look for signs that a Minotaur is occupying those woods and, when you find it, kill it. I will provide a sizeable bounty for your efforts in this matter. Do you accept this assignment?"

"Sire, can I take some time to think it over? I've never dealt with a feral Minotaur on my own before," Michael countered.

"Certainly. Take until morning and let me know what you decide. I understand this will not be an easy assignment. If you would like some backup with this matter, I can have another knight accompany you."

"What about Joshua?"

"I have word that he is currently on an assignment of his own for the Battlemages otherwise I would have called him in as well. Unfortunately, should you need backup, the bounty will have to go between the two of you. I can't be shelling out six thousand marks for a single Minotaur, no matter how menacing the bastards are."

"I understand, sire. I will consider the assignment and let you know my decision by morning time. Do you have anything else for me, Highness?"

"No. You may go. Thank you for your time, Sir Michael."

His business conducted, Michael saluted the king, bowing slightly as he clapped his first to his heart, turned sharply, and left the study before making his way out of the castle. He made his way back to Freenel Manor, his stomach growling as he walked the streets.

Chapter Three

Michael opened the front door of his knightly estate and immediately smelled a mixture of roasted herbs, meat, and spices from whatever George prepared for dinner. Michael was still not fully accustomed to having a squire at his beck and call. The first time that Michael started cooking something, George nearly lost his temper. Michael appreciated having a squire, but he still had to adjust to the life of a Knight of the Royal Order of Drendil.

"Good evening, Sir Michael," George said from the kitchen.

"George, you don't have to call me 'sir' whenever you speak to me. I want us to have an informal relationship."

"I'm sorry. It's a habit that will take some time to break. I don't mean to cause you any discomfort in my salutations."

"It's fine," Michael assured the squire.

"Coming back from the Cave?"

"The castle, actually. The king offered me an assignment."

"Oh?"

"Someone spotted what they believe is a Minotaur between Anselin and the College. His Highness asked me to find and put down this beast."

"Despicable monsters, they are. I caught a glimpse of one during the Siege and never wish to set my eyes on one again, may the Allfather grant my wish."

"That bad?"

"They're a vile mix of a man and a bull that should never have been created. I can only assume the Dark One had a hand in their spawning."

"I see. I think I'll take this assignment, though I wish Joshua could go with me. He's apparently got his own assignment for the Battlemages, though."

"Sir," George hesitated, wondering if he should speak freely, "I don't think you should go alone for this job."

"Any reason why?"

"I assume the monster will be easy enough to find, simply smell your way to it, but bringing it down may be another matter entirely. I would like to go with you for this assignment, especially after what happened with the basilisk in the desert."

"How did you learn about that?"

"Sir Joshua mentioned it after he brought you here. You were unconscious at the time. I do apologize for prying into your matters, but your livelihood is a great concern of mine as your squire. I have my assignment in this matter. I hope you understand."

"What happened with the basilisk was a fluke, George. I can assure you something like that won't happen again."

"Please, sir. I simply would like to accompany you to ensure you don't get into a situation you cannot control. It would make me feel more comfortable to go with you."

"I don't know that I want this assignment, George. I still have to think about it."

"You have said before that guard duty is growing monotonous, sir. Something like this would break that up. Besides, you haven't been on an assignment since the Manticore. Something like this would be good for you. I hope I'm not stepping beyond my reach on this."

"Not at all, George. Overseeing the patrols *has* grown tiresome. We could use the marks too. I know you have some plans for the grounds, after all."

"How many marks has His Highness offered for this?"

"Three thousand."

"That's more than enough to spruce up the grounds, sir."

Michael inhaled deeply then sighed, grabbed a bowl, and loaded meat and potatoes into the ceramic dish. "Might as well take this job then. I'll eat, then head back to the castle and speak with the king. He wanted to hear my decision before morning anyway. I'm sure he'll be happy to hear about this."

"If you would like, sir, you can write a letter to the king and I can deliver it to his courier. At least this way you won't have to leave the manor again. It will give you time to start packing supplies as well," George pointed out.

"That works for me. You're fine with walking to the castle?"

"I wouldn't have offered otherwise, sir."

"Very well. I will write a note after I eat. Did you get fresh meat today?"

"Yes, but just enough for tonight's meal. I was planning to get some salt pork tomorrow when the butcher's shop opens."

"I suppose that will have to wait."

"Certainly, sir."

Michael nodded and ate his food. George also grabbed his dinner and sat at the table to eat. Before sitting down, he retrieved the kettle from the fire and poured two cups of tea. They ate together in silence and afterward, Michael wrote a brief letter to the king explaining that he would be taking the Minotaur assignment. He sealed the letter with a glob of wax and the signet ring he acquired from Lady Sela the Gentle then handed it to George who promptly left.

Chapter Four

The next morning Michael and George rode their horses through Shemont toward the northern gate where they planned to head north on the road toward the Sorcerer's College and Anselin beyond. Flat stones, worn smooth over years of use formed the road through the city before fading entirely into packed dirt in the countryside. Michael rode a blue roan gelding by the name of Watson, while George rode a chestnut mare named Scarlet. Together the knight and his squire rode through the Drendil countryside, spurring the horses to a gallop then dropping back to a canter or trot to give their horses respites.

"Sir, I would like to speak freely with you about a matter we haven't discussed before," George said as the horses slowed to a trot again.

"Of course, George. Feel free to speak your mind."

"As your squire, it is my responsibility to look after your safety. You are not the first knight that I have served. My previous knight, and the prior occupant of Freenel Manor, was a Sir Jameson the Bear. He frequently got assignments from the king but, between them, he also enjoyed hunting for sport and food. I accompanied him on his trips, at his request. He would have me maintain a camp, cook food, and help clean the carcasses of whatever he killed during his hunting trips.

"On his last hunting trip, I was at the camp preparing food and getting ready for when he returned. He never did. I left the camp and looked for him, following the trail he had taken from the camp. After an hour I stumbled across him. He was still alive when I found him, but I couldn't do anything to save him; he had lost too much blood."

"What happened to him?"

"I asked him that very thing when I found him. What he told me is that he ran across some bear cubs and couldn't get away from them. The mother attacked him in an attempt to protect her offspring. She crushed his armor, bit and scratched him, and left him for dead after she felt he no longer posed a threat."

"I'm so sorry to hear about this, George, but is it possible that you're being a bit overly protective toward your knights?"

"To this day I am still haunted by his death. This is why I worry about you, sir. I refuse to watch another of my knights perish because of my inability to intervene. I will not allow you to face harm without doing what I can to ensure your safety.

"There's something you have to understand, sir. I was born to a family with a rich history of caring for knights. For six generations my family has squired for knights of the order. I know I was not the first in that line to lose a knight, but it pains me regardless. Sir Jameson deserved a better squire than I could have been for him. The day I returned to the city, his body on a cart, was one of the toughest of my life. I *refuse* to see that look in the king's eyes again."

"I'm sure you did everything you could for him, George."

"That's not the point I'm trying to make, sir."

"I'm sorry if I missed the point you're making here."

"It's more than fine, sir. You and I have lived vastly different lives and are in different social classes. I don't expect you to understand everything from my perspective."

"I'm sorry I failed to understand you, George," Michael said, looking down at the packed dirt road.

"If I seem too protective of you, it's simply because I cannot afford the emotional tax of losing another knight to some wild beast in a forest. That is all I had to say," George said before falling silent.

They rode in silence for a time as the woods grew closer. With the trees closing in, Michael swallowed the lump in his throat and broke the silence, though he wished he didn't have to. He felt guilty for trying to make George feel he was being too caring when that's simply how squires behave.

"We should stop to make our camp soon," Michael suggested, not meeting his squire's eyes.

"I agree," George said.

"According to the map, we should be within a day's ride of the College. I would rather avoid the Mages if at all possible. What are your thoughts, George?"

"We can ride cross-country to the west and avoid the College altogether on our way to Shaulis Woods. It should save us some time going that way as well."

"Sounds like a plan."

Chapter Five

"George, you have outdone yourself. I don't know how you can cook as well on a campfire as you can in the manor." Michael patted his stomach, pleasantly full of delicious salt-pork stew

"The concept is no different here than in our kitchen. The biggest difference here is the increased airflow around the food. It's a matter of controlling the temperature and ensuring the pot doesn't have too much heat on any one part."

"Well, regardless of how you do it, that was a wonderful meal. If you don't mind, I think I will grab some more firewood before retiring for the night."

"That sounds good, sir. I will clean up the dishes and settle into my tent for the night. If I'm not awake when you return, I hope you sleep well."

"Thank you, George."

Michael stood and walked toward the woods, stopping to secure his belt before breaking the tree line. Michael started chopping a few pieces of wood for the fire when he heard some twigs snap around him. He stopped and looked around but saw nothing in the growing darkness clinging to the woods. He heard footsteps and bestial howling nearby but shrugged and continued chopping his wood. He loaded his arms with the firewood he had cut off the fallen trees and started making his way back to camp.

As Michael rounded a tree, he heard a series of shouts and a commotion coming from the direction of their camp. He dropped the firewood, drew his sword, and rushed through the woods back toward his camp. As he ran through the woods he found a man wearing fur and leather with an axe in his hands. The man turned, hearing the sound of footsteps but only caught a glimpse of Michael before the knight's sword cut through the man's neck, his head falling to the ground and his body dropping like a sack of potatoes.

The assailant dead, Michael moved into the camp and killed another man wearing similar garb as the first. *Who are these men,* Michael thought as he looked around and saw George pinned to the ground by a third man, a large knife held to the squire's neck. George kicked and struggled against the larger man who knelt over him. Michael rushed over, kicked the man off his squire, and quickly pointed his sword toward the man's meaty neck.

"Who are you and why are you here in our camp?" Michael shouted at the man.

"We live in these woods. You're in our land," the man coughed, clutching his ribs where Michael's boot landed.

"What does that mean? Why are you here?" Michael probed.

"Those who intrude are taken to the beast," the man quivered, looking down the blade of Michael's sword.

"Do you mean the Minotaur?" Michael demanded.

The man said nothing but dissolved into maniacal laughter. Michael sighed and realized he would get nothing further from the man and buried the blade of his sword in the man's chest which ended the laughter.

George brushed dirt from his clothes as he finally stood. "Thank you, sir. Those barbarians came out of nowhere. I think we will need to move our camp come morning."

"That seems sensible," Michael panted.

"I will start cleaning these bodies out of the camp, so we don't attract any predators tonight if you're fine with that."

"Are you alright, George? I would be rattled after that experience," Michael asked.

"I seem to be fine, sir, though I'm a little shaken if anything. I will be fine once we get these bodies out of our camp."

"Let me help you with that."

Chapter Six

The songs from dozens of birds came from the trees near the camp. Michael woke up to the sound of firewood popping and the smells of food cooking over the fire. He slowly sat up, looked around, then stretched to rid his muscles of their sleepiness. As he stretched, he felt a few necessary pops in his back and shoulders, releasing a soft groan as they sounded.

"Good morning, sir. I hope you slept well and that I didn't wake you."

Michael yawned before answering. "I slept as well as can be expected in a hunting camp. You didn't wake me, George."

"Breakfast is ready whenever you want to eat."

"How did you sleep, George?"

"I couldn't sleep. Try as I might, I couldn't shake the thoughts of what happened last night. I kept hearing things moving around us and thought those barbarians would be coming back."

"I'm sorry to hear that, George," Michael said. "I wish Joshua could have joined us on this trip. He would always cast a protective spell around our camp to keep out anything that would harm us."

"I would have appreciated something like that last night. Do you think those bandits will come back?"

"I doubt they will, but we can still move the camp if you would like."

George scooped some food onto a tin plate for Michael then for himself. "I don't know if that will be necessary, sir."

Michael and George ate their breakfast in near silence. After eating, Michael reviewed his field guide once more, specifically reading over the entry on Minotaur and common habits that others witnessed among various members of the species. While the entry for the species was fairly scant of information, it at least helped Michael get a picture of where he could find this bull-man hybrid.

Chapter Seven

Michael moved cautiously through the woods, checking his surroundings as he wove between the trees deep in the woods. The layers of fallen, decomposing leaves that comprised the forest floor whispered under his boots with every step he took. As he walked through the woods, he examined the ground for signs of the Minotaur, swearing to himself for not getting more information from the marauders who had attacked their camp. They had mentioned "the beast" but he had acted too hastily when the strange man started laughing. He doubted he could have gotten any information from them, but it still felt like a wasted opportunity.

As he walked around a large, oak tree, Michael looked and found a pair of hoof prints left in the dirt. He knelt beside the prints and gently traced his fingers around the edges, finding them to be quite firm. The beast came this way, but there was no telling how long ago it was here. He looked around and found a trail of them leading toward his right. The creature must have run through the woods, given the significant gap between the hooves. He started following the tracks until they crossed another set which led back toward the center of the woods, away from the nearby College. He knelt where the paths crossed and looked in the direction where both sets of tracks led. The new set went south toward the College, but came from the north, where the other set of tracks headed. *It must live somewhere to the north of here.* He could only speculate at this point, but his instincts told him he was on the right line of thought.

The field guide described Minotaur as skittish monsters that tried their best to avoid both humans and Elves as much as they could. The entry's author briefly described the difficulty in tracking down one specimen across the Goblin Coast for over a week. Michael sighed, hoping he wouldn't have to spend as much time looking for this creature. He dreaded the thought of sleeping on the ground for that long. His back still ached from the previous night. His bedroll, while comfortable, did a poor job of competing with his stiff, supportive mattress back at Freenel Manor.

Michael stood, feeling the faintest grinding sensation in his knees, followed by a pair of crackling pops. *I'm getting too old for this kind of thing.* Years of patrolling the streets of Shemont had taken a toll on him.

Michael followed the trails going north away from the College, mindful of his footing as he moved through the woods. As he followed the trail, the ground rose slightly before cresting into a hillock. The tracks led toward the northern side of the mound and Michael followed them, hoping to find the Minotaur on the other side. He quietly drew his sword as he came to the northern edge of the hill, hearing the faintest whisper of the steel blade as it emerged from the scabbard. He watched as the strings of sunlight coming through the forest canopy reflected on the polished blade.

He continued following the trail of hoofprints around the hill until he found an entrance to a cave. Michael stood outside the cave for a few minutes, trying to see inside the dark interior. Michael knelt and inspected the dirt at the mouth of the cave which showed indents from the Minotaur's hooves coming and going. He certainly found the beast's home and now needed to find a way to lure it out. He harbored no desire to fight the creature in the dark in a habitat he didn't know.

Michael looked around and found a perfect spot to perch above the cave's mouth where he could wait for the monster to emerge. He returned his sword to its scabbard and worked his way up the hillock where he knelt on the large, flat, rocky shelf above the cave.

He knelt on the ground the way he learned while serving in the army. He sat on his feet, propped up on his toes, with his hands lying flat. One hand sat on each leg between his hips and knees, and he closed his eyes and slowed his breathing. He breathed in through his nose, held his breath for a few seconds, and exhaled softly through his mouth. As his breathing slowed he felt his heartbeat do the same. He opened his eyes and looked around, seeing only the empty forest, hearing only the sounds of birds in the trees around him. Serenity surrounded him. Tranquility. Life. Death. Balance. He waited for his quarry to emerge from the cave beneath him. Michael continued kneeling above the cave as the sun slowly worked its way toward the western horizon.

Chapter Eight

stiff breeze howled through the trees as the sun broke across the western horizon. Clouds replaced the sunlight and threatened to dump endless amounts of rain onto the earth beneath their thick, fluffy presence. Michael watched a flash of lightning split the sky and heard the peal of thunder in the distance a few seconds after. He took a deep breath through his nose and grabbed his sword belt, tying it around his waist. He grabbed his helmet, donned it, then looked toward the entrance of the cave, hoping for a sign of the Minotaur. He saw nothing but heard a heavy snorting coming from nearby.

A moment later the beast emerged from the cave, lumbering from the dark opening. Michael had no doubts he was looking at a

Minotaur as he had studied the entry in the field guide enough to recognize the bipedal man-bull creature. Michael felt his heart skip a beat as memories of his nightmares came screaming back to his mind seeing the beast. He spent many nights before the Siege of Shemont fighting a hoard of these very creatures. It stood nearly three meters tall with broad shoulders and a back that resembled a bag of ropes. Its muscles undulated under its fur-covered hide. Two curled horns protruded from each side of its head, their points reaching for the dark sky overhead.

Michael knelt on the rocky ledge for a few more moments, simply watching the Minotaur as it looked around the forest. He stood and dropped down from the ledge, falling toward the hairy beast. His boots contacted its shoulders and he felt the heavy mass of muscles crumple to the ground under him. As the Minotaur fell to the ground, Michael rolled off its back and hit the forest floor, landing on his side, and feeling his breath leave his lungs as he slammed against the ground. Both recovered quickly, and Michael drew his sword before the monster could face him.

As the Minotaur turned to face its attacker, a guttural roar came from deep within its throat. The sound echoed through the woods and birds perched in the trees fluttered off, the sound of their wings flapping drowned out by the Minotaur's grunting.

Time seemed to stop as Michael stared at the unarmed beast before him. Lightning split the sky overhead, the blue-white streak of light reflecting off the blade of Michael's sword as he held the blade out toward his foe. He took a few steps to his left, trying to circle the monster, but it turned with him. The Minotaur moved much less gracefully than Michael expected, even just to turn in a circle. It nearly tripped over its hooves at least three times in the time that it took Michael to move a couple of meters.

The Minotaur snorted once again before suddenly charging toward Michael. The knight moved to the side, letting the creature run past him before he quickly turned around to watch it as it ran through the woods and circled back. As he watched it run, he noticed it was surprisingly graceful enough not to fall over while it ran. Slow movements must be difficult for it, Michael realized.

The Minotaur turned in a wide circle and eventually came running toward Michael again, leaning forward with its head turned toward the ground. The distance between them closed much quicker than Michael anticipated though he was able to dodge to the side, swinging his sword through the air as he estimated where the monster would be. The sharpened edge met the Minotaur's left arm, slicing superficially into its hide as it ran past. Another roar came from the bull-like face as it ran past, once again running between the trees that surrounded the hillock and the Minotaur's cave.

The beast turned around much sooner this time, picking up speed as it came out of the turn. Michael could hear it breathing heavily as it raced through the trees, its hooves beating the ground as it ran toward him, still picking up speed. Michael once again moved to the side as the Minotaur approached. His sword flashed again, this time catching the beast's left leg. The beast howled and fell to the ground as the blade sliced into the muscle.

Michael watched the Minotaur tumble and come to a stop near a large oak tree. He turned, readied his sword, and watched as the creature struggled to stand. Despite the struggle it did stand and started moving toward him, limping as it moved. Blood poured from the gash in the beast's leg; hair around the wound quickly became matted from the blood and dirt. It stopped walking and quickly inspected the wound in its leg before grunting again and started to charge at Michael as he stood in the small clearing in front of the cave's entrance.

The beast closed the gap between them quickly, despite the wound in its leg. Michael dodged its massive, man-like hands as it repeatedly tried to grab him. With each attempt, Michael simply backed up and moved to one side or the other, effortlessly dodging the beast as it continued its attacks. After a few attempts to grab Michael, the Minotaur stopped and instead swung its massive hands at him, trying to knock him to the ground. Once again Michael found himself wondering why the king had issued a bounty for an unarmed creature like this, but he accepted the assignment and could only do what he came to do.

"Do you speak?" Michael asked as he dodged under another swinging arm.

He received only a panting grunt in return. He asked again as the other arm flew over his head but again got no intelligent response from the beast. Getting nothing from the monster, Michael decided not to waste any more time asking it questions. Instead, he focused on the creature itself, how it moved, the sounds of its breathing, which grew raspier the longer the fight went on, and how awkwardly it moved at slow speeds. His only experience with a Minotaur was in the nightmares he used to have about the Siege of Shemont and what little the field guide contained. He assumed this specific Minotaur was not very old, though he had no way of telling its age.

Michael swung his sword at the beast again, striking its other leg above the knee, bringing another grunting roar from the creature. As it snorted, Michael stepped forward, swinging his sword across the Minotaur's toned, muscular stomach. Blood erupted from the wound and Michael pivoted, turned to his left, and brought his sword across the back of the creature's lower legs. He heard a sickening *snap* as tendons burst under the force of the sword. The Minotaur fell to the ground, wailing as it landed with a heavy thud.

The sky above opened up and rain poured from the dark clouds as Michael stood over the wounded Minotaur. The beast started to lift itself, but Michael used his foot and pushed it back to the ground, moving toward its head. He heard the rasping breaths coming from the monster as he considered what to do next. The king gave him the task of killing this creature, and he accepted that task. He had no choice but to kill the beast, especially now that he wounded it so badly. It couldn't live on its own after this fight.

Michael raised his sword, tightening his grip on the hilt as he held the blade over his head. He inhaled sharply then brought the sword down on the back of the beast's thick neck. Bones crunched under the force of the sword. His task completed, he wiped the blood from his blade and returned the sword to its scabbard. He knelt beside the now limp body of the Minotaur, prayed to the Allfather, and grabbed his trophy by the horns before making his way back toward the camp and George.

Chapter Nine

Well done, Sir Michael," the king said, glancing at the severed head the knight held up for him.

"Thank you, sire. George and I did run into some marauders near the woods. I took care of a few of them, but the others escaped before I could deal with them."

"I'm sorry to hear that. Are you and George alright?"

"I'm fine. George is still a bit shaken, but I think being back at the manor should calm his nerves. He refused to let me go alone on this trip. He told me about what happened to Sir Jameson."

"I imagine something like that will stick with him for a while. The kingdom lost a great knight that day."

"Do you have any other assignments for me, sire?"

"Not today. Thank you for taking care of the Minotaur. As promised, here is your reward," the king said, placing a leather pouch on his desk. "You can leave the head. I will have it stuffed and hung up in the trophy room for you."

Michael set down the Minotaur's head and grabbed the coin purse. "Sire, why did it have to die?"

"It's a monster, Michael. It doesn't belong here and is a byproduct of Dark Magic, something we cannot allow to exist in our world," the king replied, not looking up from the papers on his desk.

Michael paused before speaking again. "These creatures feel pain, Highness. The Manticore looked at me before I killed it, and I swear I saw fear in its eyes."

King Orson II looked up at this. "Every mortal being fears death, Michael. It's a part of life, I suppose."

"I can understand killing the Manticore, sire. It was terrorizing villages. This Minotaur simply lived in a cave in the woods. It wasn't even armed," Michael said.

"How do we know what it could or would have done? It's easier to simply extinguish these foul creatures before they can hurt someone," the king replied, his gaze returned to his desk and the many papers scattered across it.

"Those barbarians we ran into caused more harm than the Minotaur, sire," Michael argued.

"Are you saying we should have kept it alive?" the king retorted, meeting Michael's eyes with a sharp stare.

"Respectfully, sire, I think it would have been fine to live the way it was. It wasn't hurting anyone out there in the middle of the woods. I'm not even sure how anyone spotted it, to be honest."

The king paused, taking in the knight's words. "You make a fair point. I will take that into consideration next time. Thank you, again, Michael. You have done the kingdom a service today."

His business concluded, Michael left the king's office and walked home. He passed the Cave, and though he wanted to stop inside for a quick drink, decided instead to go home and rest. He and George only spent a few days away, but he needed a good night's rest in his bed before returning to his routine the next morning.

He opened the door to Freenel Manor and smelled a wonderful symphony of spices, herbs, and meat but had no desire to eat. He wished George a good night, went to his room, and removed his armor before climbing into bed. He pulled the down-filled blanket over his head and closed his eyes, hoping sleep would come to him shortly.

Made in the USA
Middletown, DE
05 November 2023

41915499R20144